A friendship on the line . . .

"Guess what, Mona—my parents said I can compete for that prize saddle!" Ashleigh eagerly told her friend.

"Wow, so Lisa will have two of us to worry about," Mona said.

"Yeah. Isn't it great? I can't believe how mean Lisa was to you after Frisky bucked you off. That was just bad sportsmanship."

"That's all the more reason for me to beat her," Mona said. "She keeps bragging about how she's going to be the one to win the prize, but she's in for a real surprise. Now that Frisky's problem is solved, I can get down to some serious practicing. The only thing Lisa understands is winning, and I'm going to be the top rider at those shows."

Ashleigh frowned. If Mona was the top rider, then she'd win the prize. Ashleigh wanted Mona to be happy, but she also really wanted that saddle. If she was going to get it, she would have to compete seriously against her best friend. She just hoped that things wouldn't get too rough.

Collect all the books in the Thoroughbred series

Collect all the books in the Ashleigh series

* coming soon

THOROUGHBRED

Ashleigh

THE
PRIZE

CREATED BY
JOANNA CAMPBELL

WRITTEN BY
CHRIS PLATT

HarperEntertainment
An Imprint of HarperCollinsPublishers

HarperEntertainment

An Imprint of HarperCollins*Publishers*
10 East 53rd Street, New York, NY 10022-5299

This is a work of fiction. The characters, incidents, and dialogues are
products of the author's imagination and are not to be construed
as real. Any resemblance to actual events or persons,
living or dead, is entirely coincidental.

Produced by 17th Street Productions,
an Alloy Online, Inc., company

HarperCollins books are available at special quantity discounts for
bulk purchases for sales promotions, premiums, or fund-raising. For
information please call or write: Special Markets Department, HarperCollins
Publishers Inc., 10 East 53rd Street, New York, NY 10022-5299.
Telephone: (212) 207-7528. Fax: (212) 207-7222.

ISBN 0-06-009144-4

First printing: July 2002

Printed in the United States of America

Visit HarperEntertainment on the World Wide Web at
www.harpercollins.com

❖ 10 9 8 7 6 5 4 3 2 1

To my niece, Annsley Edwards, with love

1

"Oh, no!" Ashleigh Griffen groaned as she stared at the metal ring that had come loose from her English saddle's pommel. She tossed the sponge back into the bucket and stared at the old, beat-up saddle. The hand-me-down piece of equipment was almost twice as old as her eleven years, and it was really showing its age.

"Is everything okay, Ash?" Mrs. Griffen asked as she entered the barn leading Slewette, one of their brood-mares.

The bay Thoroughbred was due to foal any day now, and she was huge. Slewette huffed as she plodded down the barn aisle to her stall. Ashleigh was amazed the mare could even fit through her stall door without scraping her sides.

"I'm probably doing better than poor fat Slewette," Ashleigh teased. She pulled the D-ring from her pocket and held it up to the light. "Another piece of my saddle came loose." She saw the frown on her mother's face and decided to try to argue her case. "I really don't know how much longer this saddle will last, Mom. Don't you think it's time for a new one?"

Elaine Griffen closed the stall door behind Slewette and pulled off her hat, tucking her short blond hair behind her ears. "Ashleigh," she said with an exasperated sigh, "we've been through this before. We need every extra dime we've got to buy this new broodmare from the Millers. Your saddle had a safety check just a few months ago, and although it may look ugly, it's actually in pretty good shape. Maybe in the fall, after the yearling sale, we can pick out a new saddle." She hung Slewette's halter on the peg outside the stall door, then smiled in sympathy at her daughter.

"But it's falling apart," Ashleigh protested. She ran her fingers over the place on the cantle where the stitches were coming undone.

Mrs. Griffen studied the worn spot and nodded. "Your father and I are going to the feed store tomorrow. We'll take your saddle along and get another safety check," she said. "Maybe you'll feel better about using it if you know it's definitely safe." She gave Ashleigh a pat on the back. "You'd better bring the yearlings in and get them brushed. The Millers will be here soon. We want all of our horses to look their best."

Ashleigh pushed the saddle aside. It was a hopeless cause, anyway. No amount of saddle soap or polish would make it look any better. She went to the tack room to get the grooming box. A large bag of carrots sat on the stand by the door. She grabbed a handful to use as bribery on the yearlings. The young horses didn't always want to come when they were called, especially now, when the sweet shoots of Kentucky bluegrass were poking from the earth and the warm breath of spring blew across Edgardale's white-fenced pastures.

Ashleigh stepped from the barn and turned her face toward the growing heat of the morning sun. She paused for a moment and closed her eyes, inhaling deeply as she breathed in the scent of the clean northern Kentucky air.

She opened her eyes and couldn't help smiling despite her mood. She was so lucky to live in such an amazing place. Her family's Thoroughbred breeding farm, Edgardale, had acres of green fields that held the farm's ten broodmares, their foals, and this year's crop of yearlings. Most of the mares had foaled already, and the gangly colts and fillies nursed at their dams' sides or lay in the warm grass.

Ashleigh heard the screen door bang and looked

toward their white two-story farmhouse. Rory, her five-year-old brother, was jumping off the top step as Caroline, her thirteen-year-old sister, followed him, warning him to be careful. Ashleigh smiled as she watched red-haired Rory nod to his older sister, then turn and jump the low hedge, almost falling face first into the flower bed.

She knew her little brother was coming to help her with the horses. Rory, like everyone else in her family except Caroline, loved horses. Caro had never been bitten by the horse bug, and she spent more time trying out new styles for her long blond hair or painting her nails than riding. She pitched in and helped with barn chores because they all had to, but she didn't do much with the horses besides that.

"Ashleigh, wait up!" Rory called as he ran toward the barn. "I want to help." He caught up to his sister and gave her a toothy grin. "If I do a good job brushing the horses, can you watch me ride Moe?"

Ashleigh ruffled his hair and smiled. Moe had been hers until she had outgrown the molasses-colored pony. Then Rory had become Moe's proud owner. But her brother was still too young to be riding the cantankerous Shetland-Welsh cross by himself. "Sure— after we get done, we'll go over to the front paddock."

"Awesome!" Rory said, then turned and ran to get the grooming kits ready.

Derek Griffen joined his daughter at the yearlings' paddock. He gave a loud whistle to get the young horses' attention.

Ashleigh smiled proudly as the colts and fillies lifted their heads and whinnied, then trotted toward them. Her father was an excellent horseman. She hoped to be just like him when she grew up. People already told her how much she looked and acted like her father. She just hoped she could match his talent with horses.

"Let's halter all of the yearlings, then bring them in two at a time and put them in the small paddock by the barn," Mr. Griffen said. "I want the Millers to be able to see all of our colts and fillies up close. You and Rory can groom them in the paddock area."

They got all the yearlings moved, and Ashleigh and Rory began their grooming session.

"You missed a spot," Ashleigh said as she pointed to a big patch of caked mud that clung to a chestnut filly's side. "These horses have to look perfect for the Millers."

Ashleigh took a soft body brush and went over Wanderer's yearling filly, using quick strokes to dislodge the dust and bring out a shine on her coat. She knew how important this showing was to her parents.

Dan and Karen Miller owned a Thoroughbred mare that they were getting ready to retire from the racetrack. The eight-year-old gray, Misty Flight, had a great race record, and Ashleigh's parents said she would make a perfect broodmare for Edgardale. One of the farm's clients had already expressed a desire to purchase the first foal born from the mare if Edgardale was lucky enough to get her.

But Misty Flight came with a hefty price tag that hadn't even been settled on yet. All Ashleigh knew was that her parents wanted this mare badly, and they were going to trade one of their yearlings along with cash for the prospective broodmare.

Ashleigh finished with the black filly and went to help Rory with Althea's colt. Mrs. Griffen called out a warning that the Millers had arrived just as Ashleigh tossed the last brush into the grooming box. "Let's go meet them," Ashleigh said, grabbing Rory's hand and hurrying out to the parking area.

Mr. and Mrs. Miller were just getting out of their tan sedan when Ashleigh and Rory arrived. Caroline got there a second later. As Mr. Miller stepped out of the car, Ashleigh noticed that he was at least a head taller than her father—and her father was pretty tall.

Mrs. Miller, who had sandy hair and a nice smile, was also tall. She moved gracefully toward Mrs. Griffen with her hand extended. Ashleigh got a good feeling about her right away, and it only grew stronger when Mrs. Miller took a moment to speak with her, Caro, and Rory.

After all the introductions, Mr. Griffen motioned to the pen where all the yearlings stood with their inquisitive faces poking over the fence. "Let's get started, shall we?" he suggested.

Ashleigh and Caroline took each of the yearlings out in turn, walking and trotting them in a straight line, then holding them still for the Millers to inspect. Dan Miller asked about each colt or filly's pedigree while he ran his hands down their legs and over the tendons. Mrs. Miller looked over the yearlings, making sure there were no turned-out toes or cow hocks that might cause an infirmity when the horses began heavy race training in a year.

Mr. Miller dusted his hands on his pants after the last yearling was put back in the pen. "We've made all of our notes," he said as he shook hands with Ashleigh's parents. "We'll look over these at home, then come back on Saturday to start negotiations if that's all right with you."

Mr. Griffen nodded. "We'll look forward to seeing you." He turned to Ashleigh. "Would you please see the Millers to their car while we put the yearlings back out to pasture, Ash?"

Ashleigh nodded eagerly. She had a question she was dying to ask the Millers, but she didn't want to seem as though she was prying into their private business. She was curious about why the Millers would retire a mare with a great race record when the horse should still have several more good years left to run. Not that Ashleigh minded if it meant Misty Flight would come to Edgardale, but she still wanted to know why.

When they reached the car, Mrs. Miller spoke first. "Oh, I almost forgot. I brought some of Misty's win photos to show you." She handed the eight-by-ten color photos to Ashleigh.

Ashleigh stared at the beautiful gray mare with the black mane and tail. Misty Flight was tall and elegant, just like her owner. "She's beautiful," Ashleigh whispered in awe. She looked at one photo that showed the mare crossing the finish line alone, the other horses so far back that they weren't even in the shot. The mare ran with her ears pricked as she stretched her nose toward the finish line.

Ashleigh handed the photos back to Mrs. Miller. "I know how badly my parents want to have Misty come live at Edgardale," she blurted out. "But why would you want to retire a racehorse that's doing so well? And why wouldn't you want to keep her for yourselves?" She bit her lip, wondering if she'd been too blunt, but Mr. and Mrs. Miller just looked at her and smiled.

"We're only into the racing end of this business, not breeding," Mr. Miller explained. "And we're very small potatoes so far."

Mrs. Griffen ran her hand fondly over the win photos, then put them in the car. "We only have an acre of land, Ashleigh. I've got my riding horse, which I like to show in the summer, and we've got enough room in the barn for two racers when they're at home between race meets. We thought about trying to raise babies, but we decided that it would be better for us to stay with the racers."

Ashleigh tipped her head in confusion. "But why retire Misty at all if she's doing well?" She saw a look pass between the Millers.

"Misty hasn't been doing so well lately," Mrs. Miller said, her tone growing more serious. "Her mind just doesn't seem to be on racing anymore. Most racehorses break down or can't run anymore after a couple years of racing, so by comparison, Misty has had a pretty long and fruitful career. We don't want to make her continue to run if her heart isn't in it." She brushed her hair back from her face and sighed. "She's got one more big race left. It's a stakes race that's named in honor of my grandfather, who was a great trainer in his day."

Ashleigh saw Mrs. Miller look off into the distance, and she suddenly seemed miles away. Then she gave her head a quick shake and returned her attention to Ashleigh. "It would mean a lot to us to win that race," she said. "But at the moment we're just happy to be able to run in it. It will be Misty's last race. Then we'd like to see her retired someplace nice like Edgardale to finish out her life raising some great babies."

Ashleigh nodded in understanding. The Millers got into their car, and she waved as they drove off.

When she got back to the barn, Rory already had Moe saddled—he'd obviously been waiting for her. Ashleigh had been hoping to take Stardust for a ride, but it would have to wait until she lived up to the promise she'd made to her brother. There were a couple of hours of daylight left. She'd spend some time with Rory, then ask her parents for permission to go for a quick ride. If they said yes, she'd call her best friend, Mona Gardner, and see if she wanted to go, too.

Ashleigh spent a half hour giving Rory pointers and reminding him to keep his toes up and his heels down. When Moe started to show that he was reaching the end of his patience, Ashleigh signaled Rory that they were finished with the riding session. She turned toward the barn, in a hurry to get her own ride started. Her father and Edgardale's only hired hand, Jonas McIntire, were mixing the evening feed when Ashleigh entered the barn.

"I guess you want to go for a ride now?" Mr. Griffen said as he added a scoop of vitamins to each of the buckets. At Ashleigh's nod he motioned toward her chestnut mare, Stardust. "You were a big help today,

Ash. Have a good ride. Just be home at least half an hour before sunset."

Ashleigh ran to the barn phone to call Mona. It had been so long since she'd been riding with her friend. The spring show season was about to start, and because Mona was a serious competitor—too serious, in Ashleigh's opinion—she was always working in the arena. That meant Ashleigh rarely got to go trail riding with her anymore.

She dialed the number and waited. Mona answered after the third ring. Ashleigh quickly asked her friend about the trail ride, but she could tell what Mona's reply would be from the pause that followed.

"I'm sorry, Ash," Mona said, confirming what Ashleigh had already guessed. "But I've got a lesson over at the neighbor's farm in an hour."

Ashleigh's heart sank. "We never get to ride together anymore," she complained.

"The spring season starts next week," Mona said, her voice firm. "And Frisky hasn't been behaving very well. I need the arena work."

Ashleigh stayed silent for several moments, trying not to feel so hurt. She knew Mona loved to show her bay Thoroughbred mare. And the pair usually won lots of ribbons. It was just that Ashleigh really missed her friend.

"Why don't you meet me at the top of the field and

you can ride with me over to Theresa's farm?" Mona suggested when Ashleigh didn't say anything. "I know it's not much of a ride, but at least we'll get to talk."

"I'll meet you there in twenty minutes." Ashleigh hung up the phone and raced to get her tack and brushes.

Stardust nickered a greeting and trotted up to the fence when Ashleigh called to her. Ashleigh fed the small copper mare a carrot and ran her hand lovingly down her long white blaze. Stardust nuzzled her for another treat, but Ashleigh just laughed and pulled the halter over her head. "Come on—we've got to hurry if you want to ride with Mona and Frisky."

She led the mare back to the barn and hooked her into the crossties. Ashleigh put the saddle pad high on Stardust's withers and pulled it into place so all the hairs were smoothed in the same direction, then saddled the mare, pulling the girth snug.

She frowned at the missing parts on her saddle and the spot on the cantle where the stitching had come loose. "How about if we go out bareback a few times? Maybe that way my saddle will make it to the end of the summer," she said as she slipped the bit between the mare's teeth and pulled the bridle over her ears. She plopped her helmet on her head and led Stardust out the barn door.

Mona and Frisky were waiting for them at the edge of the field. Frisky neighed a welcome as they approached. It had been a while since the two mares had seen each other. They whuffed excited breaths into each other's nostrils, then fell into step together on the trail.

"See?" Ashleigh said. "Even Frisky thinks we don't get to ride together enough anymore." Ashleigh saw Mona frown slightly, as if to say they'd already discussed the subject once and she didn't want to do it again.

"Ashleigh," Mona said a bit impatiently, "you know how badly Lisa Martin has been teasing me lately. She's so competitive, and the only thing I can beat her at is *horses*. I've got to practice as much as I can so I can beat her this show season." She paused. "You could come take some lessons with me if you want to ride together more."

Ashleigh bumped Stardust into a trot. "You know my parents can't afford a bunch of expensive lessons," she said as she posted in time to the mare's gait. "And now it's worse than ever. They're trying to buy a new broodmare, and they don't want to spend any extra money on anything. Besides," she said, "you're the one who's going to be the great dressage rider someday, and I'm going to be a famous jockey. I need to concentrate more on racetrack things and leave the showing to you." Ashleigh smiled at her friend. "I don't know why you're worried. You know you can beat Lisa on your worst day."

Mona tightened Frisky's reins as Frisky began rooting at the bit. She frowned. "But what if I *don't* beat Lisa? She'll never let me live it down."

Ashleigh pulled Stardust back to a walk and turned in her saddle so that she could see her friend's face. "I can't believe you and Lisa used to be really good friends. Why is she so mean to you now?"

Mona shrugged. "My mom says Lisa's jealous. She's always wanted to be a great rider, but she doesn't have any natural talent. My mom thinks Lisa makes up for me beating her in the show ring by stomping me in everything else we do."

Ashleigh chuckled. "Well, she certainly beat you at sit-ups in gym class today."

Mona laughed. "I let her win that one. Who wants to do more than ten sit-ups?"

Their quick bursts of laughter startled the horses, and they had to gather their reins to keep the mares from shying.

"But I've really got to beat Lisa at the spring shows this year," Mona said with determination. "You should see the prize the horse club is giving away."

Ashleigh perked up at the mention of a prize. "What is it?"

Mona sighed dreamily. "You know that famous saddle maker from England?"

Ashleigh scratched her head as she tried to think whom Mona was talking about. Finally her face lit up in recognition. "You mean Robbie Ward? The guy who makes all of those really expensive saddles?"

Mona nodded. "The local horse club somehow managed to get hold of one of his saddles, and they're giving it away as a prize to whoever gets the most points during the spring show season. You should see that saddle, Ash," Mona said. "It's made from the best English leather, and the stirrups even have a small design of inlaid gold with the Ward name on them."

Ashleigh fingered the ragged leather of her own saddle, thinking about how great it would be to ride in a Robbie Ward saddle. "What do you have to do to win?" she asked.

"There are four shows in the spring season, and certain classes will count as point classes," Mona explained. "This Saturday is just a fun day so that everyone can get back into the swing of showing. The person with the most points at the end of the four regular shows wins the saddle."

Ashleigh smiled. "If you win that saddle, you'll get bragging rights over Lisa. She'll have to leave you alone."

"Wouldn't that be great?" Mona said with a laugh.

Then she grew serious. "The other thing is that my instructor told me I could move up to beginning-level dressage competition if I do okay in these equitation classes. That's what I really want, more than the saddle and even more than beating Lisa."

They pulled the horses to a halt in front of the riding instructor's farm. "I'll be rooting for you, Mona," Ashleigh said as she waved goodbye and turned Stardust toward home. "I know you'll do great at the shows. Just keep thinking of your dream to be a great dressage rider someday."

Ashleigh asked Stardust for a slow trot as she headed toward Edgardale. As they moved down the worn trail, she pictured in her mind's eye the Robbie Ward saddle that Mona would be competing for. She felt a small jolt of envy and almost wished she could enter the contest herself. Robbie Ward saddles were so expensive—she knew she'd never be able to afford one until after she became a famous jockey.

Stardust bobbled slightly on the trail, and Ashleigh looked up, surprised to see that they were almost halfway home. It was late in the day, and the shadows were growing long. Stardust pricked her ears and snorted as a rustling noise came from the bushes at the side of the trail.

"It's just rabbits, silly," Ashleigh said in a soothing voice, and gathered her reins. But Stardust began to sidestep as she shied away from the movement. Suddenly a small cottontail burst from the brush, cutting across their path. Stardust slammed on the brakes, staring wild-eyed at the small furry animal running down the path ahead of her, then dodged to the side.

Ashleigh grabbed for Stardust's mane, trying to regain her balance. Suddenly she heard a popping noise and felt herself slipping. She clamped her legs tight about Stardust's sides and fought to regain her balance, but too late she realized what had happened—her stirrup leather had broken, and she was sliding from the saddle with nothing to break her fall.

2

"Oomph!" Ashleigh grunted as she hit the ground and the air whooshed out of her lungs. She lay there gasping for several moments as she listened to the sound of receding hoofbeats. Stardust was going home without her. When she could breathe normally again, she rolled into a sitting position and tested her bones. She seemed to be in one piece, but she could tell she was going to have some bruises.

Ashleigh stared at her foot. The stirrup, with its broken leather, was still on her boot. She angrily wrenched the iron from her foot and glared at it. The stupid saddle had finally fallen apart. She was lucky she hadn't been seriously hurt in that fall. Maybe now she could convince her parents that she needed a new saddle.

She rose unsteadily to her feet and glared at her grass-stained clothes. Whom was she kidding? The stirrup leather breaking had been a fluke—it was something that could be fixed without tossing in the whole saddle. If her parents said they wanted her to wait until fall, she would have to wait.

Ashleigh thought about the prize saddle as she hobbled down the path. If she had that saddle, she wouldn't have to worry about pieces of it falling off. She wished that she could compete for the saddle. But showing just wasn't her thing. Besides, Stardust was only half Thoroughbred. Would she be good enough to show against the purebreds that many of the girls were riding on the local circuit? And what about her old tack? Would the others make fun of it?

As Ashleigh trudged down the path toward Edgardale, she tried to distract herself, but her mind kept returning to that prize. If she could do well in the shows she'd have a chance to win the Robbie Ward saddle. It might be worth a try. She decided to think about it overnight and talk to Mona in the morning. She could try the fun-day show this weekend, and if she did okay in that, then maybe she could compete for the saddle in the regular shows.

As Ashleigh rounded the turn, coming within view of Edgardale, she was surprised to see their old farm truck bumping roughly over the field. She halted and waved to the pickup. As it drew closer, she could see the worried expressions on her parents' faces. The truck pulled to a stop, and her mother jumped out before the dust had a chance to settle.

"Are you okay, Ash?" Mrs. Griffen asked as she turned Ashleigh around, checking for signs of injury.

Ashleigh nodded. "I'm all right," she said. "I'm just a little sore from the fall."

Mr. Griffen helped his daughter into the truck. "You really had us worried when Stardust came home alone with the saddle turned on her side."

Ashleigh held up the broken leather for her parents to see. "That old saddle finally fell apart."

Mrs. Griffen took the leather, inspecting the frayed ends of the strap. "I'll take your saddle to the tack shop tomorrow and get that safety check done again, then get some new leathers put on," she said. "If the professional says the saddle's unsafe, we'll figure a way to get you another one." She smiled and patted Ashleigh's shoulder.

Ashleigh attempted to return the smile, but she couldn't hide her disappointment. She knew what the man at the tack shop would say. Every time he checked her old saddle, he said the same thing: It was old but sturdy. He would examine it again, and if they replaced the stirrup leathers, he would say it was safe. Whether she liked it or not, if she wanted a new, expensive saddle, she was going to have to compete for it.

The following morning, Ashleigh woke up late and had to run all the way to the bus stop. She could hear the old school bus chugging up the hill as she pounded down Edgardale's long gravel driveway.

"Hurry, Ash!" Mona hollered as the bus topped the rise.

Ashleigh sprinted down the tree-lined lane, her backpack flopping on her back as she raced the bus to the bus stop.

"You made it!" Mona called just as the faded yellow bus screeched to a halt in front of them.

Ashleigh pulled her backpack off and grinned at the bus driver as she mounted the steps.

Mrs. Cecil chuckled. "I think we should enter you in the Kentucky Derby. The way you were charging down your driveway, you reminded me of one of those Thoroughbred colts you raise."

Ashleigh slipped into the seat beside Mona, huffing and puffing as she placed her backpack under the seat in front of her. She returned the bus driver's grin. "I don't think I'd do very good on foot, but someday I'm going to be a famous jockey and you'll see me riding in the Derby."

The stout, motherly driver closed the bus door with

a bang, and the bus lurched back onto the road. "I don't doubt that at all," she said with confidence. "You just follow your dreams."

They rode in silence for several minutes while Ashleigh got her breath back. She stared out the window at the oak, maple, and Bradford pear trees that had just gotten their new leaves and stood tall with their branches stretching toward the cloudless blue sky. She wished they weren't on their way to school. It was a perfect day for a ride!

As they passed one of the neighboring farms, Ashleigh leaned forward and pointed at one of the grazing horses. "Who's that?" she said, indicating the large bay horse with two hind socks and a blaze.

Mona frowned. "That must be Lisa's new horse," she said.

Ashleigh craned her neck to get a good look at the bay. *Mona's right,* she thought. *It looks like Lisa's gearing up for a season of trying to beat Mona in the show ring.*

"It's an Irish Thoroughbred," Mona said as she turned her eyes away from the horse, concentrating on the back of Mrs. Cecil's head.

Ashleigh's brows rose in curiosity. "I didn't think Lisa's mom could afford an expensive horse like that."

Mona lowered her voice, glancing around to make sure nobody was eavesdropping. "I overheard some of

Lisa's friends talking. They said her father feels guilty for not being around much, so he bought her the horse to make up for it."

"You're kidding!" Ashleigh said in disbelief. Lisa's dad must have felt *really* guilty to spend so much money on a Thoroughbred. She couldn't even get her own parents to buy her a saddle!

Ashleigh paused for a moment, glancing at Mona. "It looks like Lisa really means business."

Mona sighed and looked out the bus window. "That's what I'm afraid of."

"Don't worry," Ashleigh reassured her friend. "You're ten times better than Lisa. Irish Thoroughbred or no, she won't beat you and Frisky!"

The bus pulled to a halt in front of the school, and Mona reached for her backpack. "You're right," she said with a tremulous smile. "Lisa has never beaten me in the ring. And I'm not about to let her start. Frisky and I are going into overtime on training. Lisa won't have a chance against us!" She stepped off the bus and up the school steps, pausing at the door. "But just for fun, let's ride by Lisa's tonight while she's at rehearsal for the school play and take a look at that new horse."

Ashleigh nodded. Then she remembered what she'd meant to tell Mona first thing that day. "I might be able to help you with Lisa," she said.

Mona cocked her head. "How?"

Ashleigh opened the door to the school. The steady hum of conversation and the sound of lockers being slammed drifted out to greet them. "I've decided to join you at the show on Saturday," she said. "If I do okay, then I might ride the spring shows, too." She noticed the questioning look on her friend's face, but went on. "I figure with two of us competing, Lisa will have even less chance of winning that saddle."

Mona stood speechless for a few moments. *If I didn't know better,* Ashleigh thought, *I'd say Mona looks upset. But that doesn't make any sense—there's nothing for her to be upset about.* Then Mona nodded and stepped into the hallway, her strides so long and fast that Ashleigh practically had to run to catch up with her.

"I'll see you at lunch," Ashleigh said as she stopped outside her first class. Mona continued down the hallway. "They're serving pizza today, so try to get there as soon as you can. They always serve the burned pizzas last," she yelled after Mona.

Ashleigh went into her classroom and pulled out her book for first period. Was Mona acting funny, or was it just her imagination? Maybe Mona was still worried about Lisa's new horse. She'd talk to her about it at lunch.

•   •   •

At last the noon bell rang, and it was time for lunch. Ashleigh sprang from her chair and hurried down the hall to the cafeteria. Mona was waiting at the door, smiling, so Ashleigh figured she must have been imagining it when she thought something was wrong earlier. They gathered their trays and silverware and got into the lunch line. Ashleigh's mouth watered as they sat down at one of the long cafeteria tables. "I just love Friday— pizza day!" she said, digging into the pepperoni pizza and salad.

Mona nodded as she pulled a long string of hot, gooey cheese from the pizza and popped it into her mouth.

"Hey, Mona!"

Mona and Ashleigh's heads both snapped around at the loud voice and the sound of a lunch tray banging on the table. Lisa Martin stood there, a snide look on her face.

"I guess you won't be the only one winning blue ribbons in the show ring this year," Lisa said, grabbing her soda and slurping noisily.

"Dream on," Jamie Wilson and Lynne Duran said in unison as they joined Ashleigh and Mona at the table.

Lisa flipped her long black hair over her shoulders and glared at Ashleigh, Mona, and their friends. "Obviously you guys haven't seen my new horse," she bragged.

Jamie tossed her blond hair in imitation of Lisa. "Of course we've seen your new horse," she said. "But we've also seen you ride. I don't think Mona has anything to worry about."

"And Ashleigh told me that she's going to be showing, too," Lynne said confidently. "So you'll have all of us to compete against."

The weird look came back into Mona's eyes, and Ashleigh wished her friend wouldn't let Lisa get to her so much.

Lisa snorted. "Oh, goody," she said in a sarcastic tone. "Then I can look forward to beating *all* of you. I've seen that little mixed breed Ashleigh rides. As you can tell, I'm shaking in my boots." She picked up her tray and walked away.

"What a jerk," Lynne muttered.

Jamie nodded in agreement. "I can only stand so much of her crummy attitude. I'm glad that's the last time I have to see her today."

Ashleigh frowned and put down her piece of pizza. It didn't taste as good anymore. "Mona and I still have to deal with her in gym class."

"Just keep away from her," Lynne advised. "There are a lot of kids in that class. It shouldn't be difficult to avoid Miss Snooty."

• • •

An hour later Ashleigh and Mona discovered just how wrong Lynne could be as they faced off against Lisa in a series of tetherball games.

Ashleigh groaned in frustration as the tetherball sailed over her head and wrapped around the pole.

"I beat you, Griffen! Just like I beat your friend Mona in the last game." Lisa punched her fist in the air. "Just like I'm going to beat you both in the show tomorrow!"

Ashleigh ignored the taunts as she made her way in from the tetherball court. She turned to Mona. "I see what you mean about Lisa making fun of people. She's not very nice. I don't know if I should even bother to go to the show tomorrow," she said. "I'd really like to compete for that saddle, but what if she's right—what if Stardust and I don't have a chance against that Irish Thoroughbred? Why should I even bother to try?"

Mona handed Ashleigh her backpack, and they made their way to their last class. "I won't blame you if you decide not to go," she said, avoiding Ashleigh's gaze.

Ashleigh's eyes widened in surprise. That didn't sound like Mona. She shifted the pack to her other shoulder. "I guess I should probably give it a try first before I quit," she suggested, watching for her friend's reaction. But Mona just shrugged.

Ashleigh frowned as she walked down the hall. Why did Mona start acting weird whenever Ashleigh talked about entering the competition? Was Mona really that distracted by her anger at Lisa that she couldn't focus on anything else? Ashleigh had never seen Mona like this before, and she just hoped that whatever was wrong would get better soon.

3

Ashleigh eagerly unsnapped Stardust from the cross-ties and led her outside to the mounting block. She put on her helmet and swung into the saddle, looking forward to a relaxing ride. As she trotted down the long driveway, she could see Mona standing by the edge of the road, letting Frisky crop grass.

"I hope you didn't have to wait too long," Ashleigh said. "I had to help my parents bring the broodmares into the barn before I could go."

Mona shook her head. "I've only been here a couple of minutes, but Frisky was fidgeting, so I decided to get off and let her eat." She put her foot into the stirrup to mount, but Frisky jerked at the reins and wiggled, moving her hindquarters away from Mona so that she couldn't swing into the saddle. "Whoa!" Mona cried as she hopped on one foot, trying to get enough bounce to mount up.

"Here, let me stand Stardust on the other side of Frisky so she can't move," Ashleigh offered. She guided the chestnut mare into place and waited for her friend to climb into the saddle.

Mona mounted up, and Frisky pranced sideways for several steps, lifting her four white-stockinged legs high into the air as her tail went over her back.

"I don't know what's gotten into her lately, but Frisky hasn't been behaving very well," Mona grouched as she sawed on the reins, trying to get the mare under control. Frisky popped her head into the air, her mouth open and working as she tried to escape the pull of the bit.

"Looks like you'd better tighten your noseband," Ashleigh suggested. "Why is she slinging her head like that?"

Mona frowned. "I don't know. She just started this the other day. I don't want to get off now and go through all the trouble of having to get back on again." She gritted her teeth and worked the reins, trying to bring the mare's nose in. "Let's do some trotting and see if we can wear her down a little."

They bumped the mares into a trot. Frisky continued to fight with her rider for several more minutes, but eventually she fell into step beside Stardust and began to settle down. Ashleigh pulled Stardust to a stop when Lisa's house came into view.

"Are you sure Lisa isn't home?" she asked. "I wouldn't want her to catch us spying on her horse. She might think we're worried or something."

Mona grinned. "We *are* worried, aren't we? Isn't that the reason we're here?"

They stared at each other for a moment, then burst into a fit of giggles.

"Come on." Ashleigh looked both ways, then started Stardust across the road. "Let's go see this horse that's going to make Lisa a star rider this year." She glanced sideways at Mona, and they burst into another peal of laughter. "That gelding would have to be Superhorse to carry Lisa to a blue ribbon," Ashleigh said with more confidence. But a moment later, when the Irish Thoroughbred came across the pasture at an extended flat-kneed trot, his neck bowed in a perfect arch, Ashleigh felt a pang of doubt.

Mona let out a long, low whistle of appreciation. "I think we've just met Superhorse, Ash. Look at the way he floats over the ground."

Ashleigh nodded. Mona was right—the horse was perfect.

The big bay gelding stopped at the fence with his broad chest pushed up against the white boards. He swished his long black tail and nickered a greeting to the two mares. Stardust tried to crowd closer to touch noses with the handsome gelding, but Ashleigh pulled on the reins, asking the chestnut to back up a step.

"Oh, no you don't," she cautioned the mare. "Touching noses helps spread germs, and that horse has just been shipped here. I don't want you getting sick if he's carrying something."

"Wow," Mona said as she studied the horse. "All Lisa will have to do is stay in the saddle, and this horse will carry her to a ribbon."

Ashleigh frowned as she shifted in her beat-up saddle. She and Stardust didn't stand a chance of winning against a horse like this. She should just tell Mona right now that she was pulling out of the show. Mona probably wouldn't mind, since she didn't seem to be too enthusiastic about Ashleigh attending the show with her on Saturday, anyway.

She glanced at Mona and thought about how much fun she had when they went riding together. They didn't get to do it as often anymore, now that Mona was so busy with her lessons. Maybe she should forget about winning the saddle and just go have a good time with her best friend and her horse.

"Let's get out of here before Lisa pulls up and catches us gawking like a bunch of bug-eyed toads," Ashleigh said.

They turned the horses and headed toward home,

making plans to get up early the next day. They wanted to get to the show arena early so Mrs. Gardner could get a good parking spot for the horse trailer.

"Are you sure it's okay that I go with you to the show?" Ashleigh asked as they neared home. "You don't seem like you're very happy about me going."

Mona hesitated, then gave Ashleigh a smile. "No, it's okay, Ash. I'm sorry I've been so grouchy lately, but Lisa is really bugging me. I just *have* to beat her at this." She sat up straighter in the saddle. "I want to be a champion dressage rider one of these days," she said. "How can I make that happen if I can't even beat stupid ol' Lisa?"

Ashleigh nodded in understanding and bumped her mare into a trot. Stardust behaved like a lady the entire way home, but Frisky got worse the closer they came to Edgardale. When the farm came into view, the bay mare began tossing her head in the air as she trotted sideways down the path. Mona pulled sharply on the reins, trying to force Frisky into a tight circle, but the mare slung her head from side to side, trying to rid herself of the pressure on her mouth.

"I said *whoa!*" Mona spoke through clenched teeth as she gave one big pull on the reins.

Suddenly the mare dropped her nose to the ground and crow-hopped. "Hold on!" Ashleigh called to Mona as she gave Stardust a nudge, hoping she could move in and grab a rein before Mona came off.

Frisky was heading toward the fence at the edge of the road. She stopped right before hitting the rails, and Mona lost her stirrups, sliding forward onto the bay's neck.

Ashleigh leaned far out of the saddle to snag one of the loose reins. Frisky snorted and tried to pull away, but Ashleigh held on tight, waiting for Mona to right herself in the saddle. "Are you okay?" she gasped.

Mona gathered her reins and brushed the hair from her eyes. Her cheeks were two red blotches in the middle of her ashen face. "I—I think so," she stammered. She dismounted and stood on shaking legs. "I don't know what got into her. Maybe she spooked at something."

Ashleigh scrunched her lips. "That didn't look like a spook to me," she said. "Frisky looked like she was trying to get rid of you on purpose. Maybe I should pony you home?"

Mona shook her head. "We're almost there. I'll just walk her back to my place."

Ashleigh dismounted. "Are you sure you're okay?" At Mona's nod, she turned Stardust, and they walked the mares toward Mona's house.

Mona waved goodbye at the top of the driveway. "We'll pick you up at seven tomorrow morning. I'll see you then."

Ashleigh watched them go. Something was up with

Frisky. It wasn't like the mare to behave so badly. She hoped Mona didn't get hurt before she figured out what the problem was.

The show grounds were a hive of activity, with riders running here and there to get their numbers and register for classes. Horses stood tied to trailers, waiting to be saddled or, if they were in a later class, enjoying their breakfast.

Stardust stood tied to the trailer with her ears pricked, watching all that went on around her. She snorted and danced around, refusing the food in her hay net. Frisky remained calm, lazily munching her hay as the activities carried on. It was obvious which horse was the most experienced at the show routine.

Ashleigh was glad to see that Frisky was behaving herself. She didn't want to see a repeat of what had happened the day before. The next time, Mona might not be so lucky.

"It looks like we weren't the only ones who wanted to get here early," Mona said as she pulled the new saddle she had received for Christmas out of the tack compartment of the trailer.

Ashleigh picked up the box of grooming brushes and nodded. "If we'd gotten here ten minutes later, we'd be parked pretty far away." She gave Stardust a good grooming and then pulled her tack from the rig. She frowned at the ragged saddle. It looked a little better—Rory and Caroline had helped her polish it and make some small repairs the night before. They really wanted her to do well at this show. She had tried to explain to them that she didn't stand a chance, but they didn't believe her. She smiled inwardly. It was nice to know her family had faith in her abilities. She just wished she had as much faith in herself.

Mona placed her white quilted saddle pad on Frisky's back and set the saddle in place. "Let's get the horses saddled and then go up to the office for our show numbers," she said. "We're only going to have a short while to warm up."

They hurried to the office and retrieved their competition packets.

"Look," Mona said. "There's a discount coupon for the tack store in our class registration packet, and another for a free small bag of horse treats. We'll have to go there after the show."

They headed back to the trailer, where Mrs. Gardner was watching the horses. "We'd better hurry," Ashleigh said. "The first class is the walk-trot class. It'll probably be the only one I've got a chance to ribbon in."

They bridled the mares and mounted up. Mrs. Gardner took a damp cloth and wiped off the dust that had accumulated on their shiny black boots. When she was sure they both were ready, she shooed them off to the warm-up pen.

Mona pointed to the warm-up area as they approached. "Lisa's on her old horse, and her trainer, Pam Ridel, is riding the new one. I wonder what's up."

Lynne and Jamie were already trotting around the pen when Ashleigh and Mona entered. They slowed their mounts and walked a warm-up lap with the girls. Ashleigh tried to fan her coat over the back of her saddle so that the other girls wouldn't see where the stitching had come loose.

Jamie waited until they had passed Lisa and her trainer, then leaned toward the others and spoke in a low voice. "I heard Lisa can't handle her new horse yet, so her trainer is going to ride him in a couple of classes."

"Great!" Mona grouched sarcastically. "Now we have to compete against a professional."

Jamie clucked her gelding into a faster walk to keep up with the other horses. "The good thing is that Pam is only showing Ranger in a couple of classes. But Lisa will be in all the classes with old Rusty, and all of us have beaten them before. I don't think Lisa's going to be a problem."

They broke the horses into pairs, trotting around the warm-up ring. Stardust snorted and tossed her head, while Frisky moved quietly beside them. Ashleigh was happy for Mona, but she was starting to worry about her own horse.

It wasn't long before they heard the call for the first class. Everyone filed out of the gate and waited to be let into the main arena. Stardust stomped her hoof and shook her head, eager to be on the move. Ashleigh put a steadying hand on the reins.

"Is she going to be all right?" Mona asked.

Ashleigh shrugged. "It's been a while since Stardust has seen this much activity. She's pretty excited."

Mona smiled sympathetically. "Maybe she'll settle down once we're inside and moving." She was about to say more when Frisky was jostled from behind as Lisa and Rusty squeezed their way through the crowd of horses.

"I just wanted to wish you girls luck," Lisa said in a falsely sweet voice. She paused for emphasis, looking at each of them down the length of her sharp nose. "You're going to need it!" she finished with a self-assured laugh.

"Riders, please enter the ring at a trot," the show steward called.

Ashleigh waited until the riders in front of her moved. Then she clucked to Stardust and entered the ring on the rail at a trot. Stardust flipped her head around, and Ashleigh did her best to bring the mare's nose in before the judge looked in her direction. They circled the ring twice before the judge asked for a halt and a reverse into a walk. When they trotted again, Stardust didn't want to collect herself. The mare stepped out at an ungainly trot.

"There's one rider I don't have to worry about," Lisa said with a laugh as Ashleigh and Stardust flew past them.

Ashleigh frowned as she worked the reins, collecting her horse slowly so the judge wouldn't see a sudden change of pace, but they passed several horses on the inside before she got Stardust slowed down. One of the horses was Frisky.

"Take it easy, Ash," Mona whispered loudly.

Ashleigh noticed that Frisky looked calm and was performing well. Stardust settled down once she was near her friend. They trotted at an even pace in front of Mona and Frisky.

Ashleigh cut her eyes to the center of the ring, where the judge stood writing on his clipboard. She hoped he wasn't making notes on her, but she was sure their uncontrolled gait hadn't escaped his attention.

The judge lifted his clipboard, signaling that he was ready for the riders to pull in and line up. Ashleigh stood Stardust next to Frisky. She backed without difficulty when the judge came to her. Then they stood and waited for the man to hand in his results.

Did he notice our wild pace? Ashleigh wondered as she waited for the results. Stardust hadn't been out of control for that long. Maybe the judge hadn't seen them.

"We have our winners of the walk-trot class," a woman's clear voice said over the loudspeaker system. "In first place is number two twenty-two, Pam Ridel, aboard Ranger!"

Ashleigh admired the big bay as he walked gracefully forward and stopped while his rider collected the ribbon.

"In second place," the announcer continued, "is number one twenty-four, Mona Gardner, riding Frisky."

Ashleigh clapped happily for her friend. But she scowled a moment later when Lisa's name was called for third place.

Lisa rode by with a too-wide smile pasted on her face. "Guess that's one for me and none for you," she said snidely to Ashleigh as she trotted by.

Much to Ashleigh's surprise, her number was called for a fifth-place ribbon. She sat there for a moment, not sure she had heard correctly. A short whistle from Jamie brought her out of shock, and she moved forward with a big smile to collect her ribbon. The judge must not have seen her struggle with Stardust, she mused.

Ashleigh was pleased when she and Stardust placed in the English pleasure and hunt seat classes. Mona, Jamie, Lynne, and Lisa also placed in several more classes. She began to think that she might actually be able to compete for the prize saddle.

"We're doing good," Mona said when they tied the horses to the trailer, letting them eat during the fifteen-minute break before the English equitation class. "Lisa hasn't beaten me in a single class."

Ashleigh smiled. "This show has been kind of fun," she admitted. "Except for stupid Lisa being such a pain."

Mona removed Frisky's bridle and loosened the girth on the saddle. "Miss Lisa," she said in a sarcastic tone, "isn't doing as well as she hoped. If I can win a couple of classes, I'll have a big mental jump on her before she starts competing with Superhorse."

Ashleigh took the soft body brush and ran it over Stardust's shiny coat. "The equitation classes are usually my best. Maybe I can win one of them," she said wistfully.

Mona didn't respond, keeping her eyes on Frisky.

Ashleigh paused with her brush in midair and glanced at Mona. Why did her friend keep acting so moody?

Ashleigh finished with Stardust and gratefully accepted the bag of chips and soda that Mrs. Gardner handed her.

"You two had better eat quickly," Mrs. Gardner warned. "You only have a few more minutes until they call for your next class."

The girls turned over feed buckets and sat in the warm spring sunshine while they enjoyed their snack. Five minutes later the first call for the English equitation class came. They tossed their garbage in the trash bag inside the truck and went to get the mares ready.

"Oh, no!" Mona cried. "Look at my bridle." She held it up for Ashleigh to see. Frisky had chewed the leather on the cheek strap.

"How did that happen?" Ashleigh looked at the damage and shook her head. "There's no way you can hide that from the judge. Did you bring another bridle?"

Mona nodded. "It's the old one I use for trail rides, but it should be okay for this." She frowned. "I guess I hung the bridle too close to Frisky, but she's never chewed on it before."

The announcer's voice came over the speaker. "This is your five-minute call for class number twelve, English equitation. Riders, please report to the gate in five minutes."

Mona hurried to find the other bridle. Ashleigh got Stardust ready, then went to see how her friend was doing.

"What can I do to help?" she asked.

Mona pulled the bridle over Frisky's ears and buckled the throatlatch. "I think I've got it," she said as she tightened the girth on her saddle. "But I—ouch!"

"What's the matter?" Ashleigh looked over the top of her saddle to see Mona rubbing her arm.

"Frisky nipped me when I tightened the girth," Mona said in surprise.

Ashleigh buckled her helmet and prepared to mount up. The other riders were already gathering at the entrance gate. "Maybe the girth pinched her, or maybe there's something stuck on it," she suggested. "You'd better hurry and look. They'll be calling us to the gate any second now."

Mona checked the piece of equipment but couldn't find anything wrong. She mounted up just as the announcer called all entrants to the arena. She turned Frisky in a tight circle to fall in behind Ashleigh, and the mare flipped her head in the air, almost hitting Mona in the face.

"What's wrong with you?" Mona said to Frisky as she fought to get the mare under control.

"Is she going to be okay?" Ashleigh asked, concerned about the sudden change in Frisky's behavior. She was acting the same way she had the other day when she had tried to buck Mona off. "Maybe you should sit this class out and take Frisky to the warm-up pen to work her kinks out."

They approached the gate, and the show steward

waved them in. "Numbers one twenty-four and one twenty-five, you're the last two to fill out the class. Let's go!"

Frisky barged through the entrance ahead of Stardust. The bay mare shook her head several times as Mona tried to steer her closer to the rail. Stardust pricked her ears in interest.

"Oh, no you don't," Ashleigh said as she guided the little mare past her struggling friend. "You're not going to follow Frisky and blow this class. Mona will get her straightened out. You just concentrate on doing what I ask."

Ashleigh sat straight in the saddle, concentrating on keeping her lower legs still and her heels down. Out of the corner of her eye she could see the judge watching her. She spotted Mona on the opposite side of the ring. At least Frisky seemed to have settled down.

The judge asked for several different gaits, then instructed the riders to drop their stirrups. This part always made Ashleigh nervous. If Stardust decided to act up while she was riding with her feet out of the irons, Ashleigh would be at the mare's mercy. Her legs just weren't long enough to wrap around the chestnut's rib cage if the mare decided to buck.

After what seemed like an eternity at the canter with no stirrups, the judge asked the horses to line up. This time Mona was at the opposite end of the arena.

Ashleigh winced when she noticed Frisky fussing again. She could tell by the look on Mona's face that there would be no ribbon for Frisky in this class.

"The results are in," the announcer said. "And the first-place ribbon goes to number one twenty-five, Ashleigh Griffen, riding Stardust!"

Ashleigh gasped in surprise. She knew she and Stardust had done well, but she hadn't expected to win. She glanced quickly toward the other end of the lineup and felt a jolt of hurt at the big frown on her friend's face. But as soon as Mona noticed Ashleigh's gaze, she flashed a smile and gave Ashleigh a thumbs-up sign.

Ashleigh returned the smile and asked Stardust for a walk, reining her toward the judge who was giving out the ribbons. She leaned down to accept her first blue ribbon of the season.

At the sound of a desperate cry, Ashleigh's head snapped around. She watched in horror as Frisky ran full speed across the arena, heading straight for the opposite fence.

4

Ashleigh watched helplessly as Frisky galloped across the arena with her head high in the air. Mona was standing in the irons and pulling on the reins while the mare shook her head from side to side as if to spit out the bit. She could hear the gasp of the crowd as the runaway mare neared the fence.

"Mona!" Ashleigh screamed. "Get her turned or stop her!"

A spectator standing by the rail quickly climbed the fence and began waving his arms, trying to prevent the mare from hitting the fence. The man, who was wearing a loud red shirt, must have gotten Frisky's attention, because the mare suddenly cut to the right and screeched to a halt, sending her rider over her shoulder. Mona hit the ground with a loud thud and rolled in the dirt.

Ashleigh shoved her blue ribbon into the pocket of her riding jacket and booted Stardust into a canter. She rode to Mona's side and flew out of the saddle before Stardust had come to a full stop. "Are you all right?" she cried as she looked into Mona's dirt-smudged face.

Mrs. Gardner ran into the arena, kneeling at her daughter's side. Mona sat up, but a paramedic arrived on the scene and asked her to lie back down until he could check to make sure she didn't have any serious injuries.

The ring steward brought Frisky back, and Ashleigh held both mares while she waited for the medic to examine Mona. After several minutes he helped her to her feet and turned to Mrs. Gardner.

"She seems to be fine—just a few bumps and bruises," the medic said. "I don't think she should ride anymore today, though," he advised. At Mona's stricken look, he shook his head. "I'm serious, young lady. You're very lucky you didn't break anything in that fall. I want you to stay off the horses until tomorrow at the earliest. The veterinarian will be over to check your horse in a few minutes. Go back and get her untacked."

Mona sighed and took Frisky's reins from Ashleigh. She handed her helmet to her mother and led Frisky from the ring with her head bowed in defeat. Ashleigh followed with Stardust.

"Are you sure you're okay?" Ashleigh asked as they tied the horses to the trailer and she helped Mona untack her mare.

Mona rubbed her bruised hip and nodded. "Yeah, but I kind of hurt all over. I'll be back in action by tomorrow. I just wish I could have beaten Lisa in a few more classes." She pointed to the ribbon sticking out of Ashleigh's pocket. "Congratulations on winning first place. You deserved it."

Ashleigh took the blue ribbon from her pocket, smoothing out the wrinkles. "Thanks," she said. "I'm still not sure I'm good enough to win the saddle, but I guess it's worth a shot."

"So you're going to ride the entire spring season?" Mona asked, not looking at her friend.

Ashleigh nodded. She watched as Mona pursed her lips and paused for a moment before speaking.

"Good," Mona said as she loosened Frisky's girth.

But Ashleigh saw the way Mona's eyes avoided hers, and she wondered if Mona was upset.

"You've got five minutes until the green-hunter-over-fences class starts," Mona said as she slipped the saddle from Frisky's back. "You'd better hurry."

Ashleigh bit her lip, deciding not to push Mona about why she was acting weird. She was probably just upset about her spill. Ashleigh took the bridle Mona slipped over Frisky's head and hung it in the tack compartment. "I thought I'd stay here and make sure you were all right."

Mona made a shooing motion. "I've already got one mother here to watch over me," she said with a laugh as she accepted a wet washcloth from her mother to wipe away the dirt on her face and hands. "Go ahead. Mom and I will watch you from the fence. I want to see you and Stardust trounce Lisa."

As if on cue, Lisa rode past while Ashleigh was checking Stardust's equipment.

"That was quite a show, Mona," Lisa said with a snicker. "Looks like maybe we can count you out of the running for the saddle. I don't think they give points for stunt riding." She laughed hard at her own joke, ignoring Mona's hurt expression.

Ashleigh glared at Lisa's back as the black-haired girl trotted away. "Don't pay any attention to her, Mona." She put her foot in the stirrup and mounted. "She's just a brat with a big mouth. Everyone here knows you're a much better rider than Lisa."

Mona put her saddle into the trailer and frowned. "You wouldn't know it after that last stunt Frisky pulled." She placed her hands on her hips. "I don't know what's going on with this mare, but I'm not going to let Lisa get the best of me. Frisky and I are going to work twice as hard so that we can beat Lisa!"

The call to the ring came, and Ashleigh turned Stardust toward the arena. She glanced back, noting the sad look on her friend's face. This was the last class she really needed to be in—the rest were just fun classes that she and Mona had entered to have a good time. She could miss the egg-and-spoon race and the bareback dollar-bill event. Mona was probably in pain and anxious to go home.

Ashleigh entered the ring at a walk and surveyed the two low jumps in the middle of the ring. Stardust had jumped higher things than that in the field. Maybe she'd have a chance at placing in this class.

The judge ran the eight competing horses through all of their gaits before they were called individually to take the two jumps. Ashleigh waited patiently while several of the competitors had their turns. She was the fifth to go on the short course. She leaned down and patted Stardust. "Let's do this right, girl," she said. "I know we haven't jumped for a while, but they aren't very high. Just listen to what I tell you."

Ashleigh walked her mare from the lineup, then cantered her in a large, slow circle, studying the jumps before heading toward the first one. She judged her distance, leaning slightly forward and squeezing with her legs as she asked Stardust to take off several feet before the low rail. Stardust sailed over the jump, landing lightly.

Ashleigh felt the mare start to pick up speed as her

ears pricked toward the next hurdle. She gathered the reins, asking Stardust to listen for instructions. The mare obeyed and lessened her pace. Ashleigh judged the next jump, but she got a little excited and asked Stardust to take off too soon. The little chestnut responded on cue and took off several feet before she should have, but she cleared the jump with no faults. Ashleigh smiled happily as she trotted back to join the others.

"Way to go, Ash!" Mona shouted from the bleachers.

Ashleigh smiled. Mona seemed to be back to her old self.

The next team to go was Lisa and Rusty. The girl gave her a haughty smile as she walked her gelding from the lineup.

Ashleigh didn't want to wish any rider bad luck, but if anybody deserved it, it was Lisa. She glanced over her shoulder to Mona and winked. They both knew Rusty was a lousy jumper. She wasn't sure why the girl was acting so smug.

Lisa put the gelding into a slow, lumbering canter. It looked as if the old horse needed every ounce of energy he could muster just to maintain the pace. Ashleigh wondered how he was ever going to make it over the fences.

She watched as Lisa nudged Rusty's head several feet before the first jump and gouged him in the sides to get him to leap. The old gelding was so surprised, he popped straight up and cleared the first jump, landing heavily on the other side. When they came to the second jump, Lisa tried the same tactic, but the wise gelding broke his canter and trotted sloppily over the second jump, knocking down the poles as he went.

Ashleigh tried to hide her smirk. She knew it wasn't nice to be happy that Lisa had messed up, but Lisa certainly never worried too much about being nice.

Jamie and Lynne were the last two to go, and they both had good runs also. Ashleigh gave them a thumbs-up as they all rode into the center of the ring to line up for the results.

Her friends were awarded first and second place. Ashleigh was clapping happily and almost missed the announcement that she had won the third-place ribbon. She smiled and bent to hug Stardust before moving forward to collect the white ribbon.

Mona was waiting for her at the gate. "All three of you beat Lisa!" She beamed and slapped Ashleigh a high five.

"This is going to be my last class," Ashleigh said, happy to see Mona smiling again. "We can leave as soon as the vet is done looking at Frisky."

"Dr. Markel said he'd wait until we finished watching you in this class. I'll be right over as soon as I tell Lisa what a great job she did!" Mona laughed.

Ashleigh looked to where the ring steward stood a

few feet away. "Don't get yourself in trouble for bad sportsmanship," Ashleigh whispered.

"I won't say anything bad," Mona assured her. "I just think it's Lisa's turn to hear someone brag a little."

Ashleigh grinned. "I'll see you back at the trailer."

The veterinarian was waiting with Mrs. Gardner when Ashleigh jumped off Stardust. "Mona will be here in just a minute," she said.

Dr. Markel grabbed his stethoscope. "I'll get started."

As Ashleigh untacked Stardust, she watched the vet. The man went over every inch of the mare. Mona arrived just as he finished running his hands over each of Frisky's legs.

"Is she okay?" Mona asked.

Dr. Markel straightened and dusted off his hands. "I can't find anything wrong."

Mona pursed her lips and shoved her hands into her pockets. "This is the second time Frisky has acted up with me this week. What could be causing it?"

"Her behavior doesn't seem to be caused by any unsoundness," Dr. Markel said. "Have you checked your saddle pad to make sure there's nothing sticking her? And what about your bridle?"

Mona retrieved the equipment from the tack compartment of the trailer. She handed the bridle to the vet and checked the saddle pad herself. "I don't feel anything," she said.

Dr. Markel studied the bridle for a few moments, scratching his chin as he turned the bit back and forth under the bright sun. He ran his thumb over the metal. "I may have something here," he said. "Feel this." Ashleigh was standing closest, so he handed the bridle to her.

"Ouch!" Ashleigh cried in surprise as her thumb scraped across the metal burr on the part of the snaffle that crossed the horse's tongue. She gave the bridle to Mona.

"Wow," Mona said. "No wonder Frisky was fighting the bit." She turned to the vet. "This is the same bridle I had on her when she tried to buck me off the other day. But how could it get this sharp point on it? I haven't done anything to make it like this."

Dr. Markel packed his things to go. "Sometimes equipment wears funny," he said. "That's why you should always check your tack. You were very lucky that you didn't get badly hurt today."

"Will Frisky be okay to ride tomorrow?" Mona asked.

Dr. Markel pulled Frisky's head from her hay net and opened the mare's mouth to inspect it. "I don't see any lacerations," he observed. "She should be okay for riding. Just make sure *you're* ready to get back in the saddle. That was quite a fall you took today."

Mona nodded. "Thanks, Doc. I hope we've got the problem solved, so this won't happen again." She unhooked Frisky and opened the trailer door. "Let's load them up. I think I've had enough excitement for one day."

Ashleigh loaded Stardust in the trailer after Frisky. They checked to make sure all their gear was packed, then headed for home. Ashleigh smiled at the five ribbons she had won. She was starting to think that maybe she had a chance at the saddle. The rest of the way home, she and Mona made war plans to beat Lisa at the next show.

"Looks like you've got company," Mrs. Gardner said as they pulled into Edgardale to let Ashleigh and Stardust off.

Ashleigh brightened. "That's the Millers. They've got a nice racehorse that my parents want to buy and retire as a broodmare. With all of the excitement of the show, I forgot they were coming today."

She hopped out of the truck as soon as it came to a stop, and waited for Mona to help her unload Stardust. "I'll call you later and let you know if they made a deal," Ashleigh told Mona. She waved as they headed back out the driveway.

Jonas rounded the corner of the barn and came to help Ashleigh with her mare. "Let me put this horse away while you take care of your equipment," he offered.

Ashleigh handed the old groom the lead rope. "What's happening?" she asked.

Jonas tipped his hat back. "They've been in there for almost an hour," he said as he shook his graying head in dismay. "That's not a good sign. If they had a deal, they would have come out by now."

Ashleigh cringed. "I know how badly Mom and Dad want this mare," she said. "Misty has the bloodlines they've been looking for. I heard my dad talking to Mr. Danner in Florida last night, and Mr. Danner said he'd be willing to buy Misty's first foal if we get her." At Jonas's knowing grin, Ashleigh felt herself blush. Jonas was well aware of her problem with eavesdropping.

The old groom chuckled as he turned and walked Stardust toward the front paddock. He called back over his shoulder, "I've always said that if you want to know about something, go ask Ashleigh!"

Ashleigh couldn't help but laugh with the old stable hand. But a moment later the smile came off her face when her parents and the Millers emerged from the barn. The look on her parents' faces told her that the negotiations hadn't gone well.

5

Ashleigh could barely wait as she stood there watching her parents shake hands with the Millers. She *had* to know what had gone wrong. Mrs. Miller waved goodbye to her as she and her husband headed to their car, and Ashleigh raced over to her parents.

"What happened?" Ashleigh asked her mother.

Mrs. Griffen sighed. "We couldn't come up with enough cash, and they didn't want to take two of the yearlings in trade," she said.

Ashleigh turned to the Millers. Mr. Miller was just opening the door for his wife. She knew she had to think of something quickly. Once the Millers drove away, that would be the end of it. "Wait!" she cried as she ran toward the car.

Mrs. Miller stepped back with an alarmed look on her face. "What's the matter?" she asked.

Ashleigh took several deep breaths and tried to steady her heart rate. "There's got to be a way to make this work," she pleaded. She paused, her mind racing, and remembered what the Millers had said to her the last time they were here. "You said Misty was in trouble and you didn't expect her to do very well in her last race, right?" The Millers exchanged confused glances, then nodded at her. Out of the corner of her eye she saw her parents striding toward them, and she rushed on. "Edgardale has worked miracles with a couple of troubled horses. Maybe we could do the same for Misty."

She could hear the crunch of her father's boots on the gravel driveway, and she knew she had only seconds left. "Since you're not expecting Misty to win anyway, maybe if we trained her and she won, you'd consider the win purse as part of the money my parents are missing to buy Misty," she blurted out.

"Ashleigh, what are you doing?" Mrs. Griffen said as she and Ashleigh's father came up next to them.

Mr. Griffen put a firm hand on his daughter's shoulder. "We apologize," he said to the Millers. "Ashleigh just loves racing so much that sometimes she gets a little carried away and opens her mouth before she thinks things through."

Ashleigh felt the squeeze of her father's hand on her shoulder, and her stomach did a little flop. She was in big trouble.

Mr. Miller leaned his tall, lanky form against the car and scratched his chin. "Now, just a minute, Derek," he said as he tilted his head and studied Ashleigh. "Your daughter has a decent idea there. We've got nothing to lose by trying her plan."

Ashleigh's father released his firm grip on her shoulder, and she breathed a small sigh of relief.

"You know I'm not a trainer myself," Mr. Griffen said. "But we've got a friend named Mike Smith who is a very good trainer. I'll have to give him a call and see if he can help out."

Mr. Miller nodded. "However you want to work it," he said. "If you think this could really work, I'd like to give it a try. It would mean the world to my wife and me if Misty could do well in her last race."

Mrs. Miller laid a hand on her husband's arm and smiled. "If Misty did manage to win this race, the winner's share of the purse would more than make up the difference in her sale price."

"Let me place a quick call to Mike," Ashleigh's father said. "I'll be right back."

The rest of them stood in the driveway, waiting, as he disappeared inside to make the call. Ashleigh could feel everyone's eyes on her. The Millers seemed mostly amused, but Ashleigh could tell by the quirk of her mother's eyebrow that she was in a lot of trouble once their guests left. She crossed her fingers that Mike would say yes to helping with Misty and that everything would work out.

A few minutes later Mr. Griffen walked out from the barn with a broad smile. "Looks like everything's okay," he said to the Millers. "If you'll please step back into my office, we can work out the details of when the mare can be delivered to Edgardale."

Ashleigh fell into step behind the Millers, but her mother spoke up. "I believe you have some stalls to finish," she said, giving Ashleigh a pointed look.

Ashleigh turned and headed for the wheelbarrow and pitchfork. She kept busy with the stalls until she heard the Millers' car drive off. Then she dumped the last wheelbarrow load and hurried over to her parents' office.

"Come in, Ash," Mr. Griffen said when he saw her peeking around the corner.

Ashleigh stepped into the office and jammed her hands into her pockets, waiting for her lecture.

Elaine Griffen cleared her throat from her perch on the edge of the desk. "Well, the good news is that everything worked out, and Misty will be delivered here tomorrow. Mike will stop by and help us with the training."

Ashleigh stared at her mother. She knew there was more.

"But Ash, even though it was all okay this time, you really shouldn't interfere in these things. Luckily the Millers didn't mind, but some people might have been uncomfortable with your suggestion and not known how to react."

"But it all worked out for the best," Ashleigh protested. "We're getting a second chance to buy Misty Flight. Isn't that what everyone wanted?"

Mr. Griffen signaled for Ashleigh to take a chair beside him. "Look, Ashleigh, we know that you had your heart in the right place, but the point your mother and I are trying to make is that you should think things through a little better. You could have run the idea by us first and let *us* suggest it to the Millers."

Ashleigh bit her bottom lip and nodded. "I know. I'm sorry."

Her mother gave her a quick hug. "Just take a few moments and think before you do some of the crazy things you do, Ash." She gave her a nudge toward the office door. "Of course, you do know that you're going to be helping a lot with the training and care of Misty?"

Ashleigh nodded eagerly. "Is that my punishment?"

Mr. and Mrs. Griffen laughed.

"It was meant to be," her father said. "But somehow I get the feeling that *punishment* isn't exactly the right word."

Ashleigh ran out the door to prepare the stall for Misty Flight. Things were going to work out. She just knew it!

That night at dinner Ashleigh tried to be helpful to everyone. It was her way of saying she was sorry. She helped Caroline with the spaghetti and set the table without having to be asked. Rory helped her butter the bread for garlic toast, but he managed to get more butter on himself and the countertop than on the bread.

When the family finally sat down to dinner, Ashleigh felt a certain amount of pride in having helped prepare the feast.

"Let's eat!" Rory declared as he eyed the big bowl of spaghetti.

Everyone passed the dishes and filled their plates. Mrs. Griffen placed a piece of garlic toast on Ashleigh's plate. "With everything we had going on today, I didn't get the chance to ask you how your show went, Ash," she said.

Ashleigh twirled her fork in the long noodles, winding them into a ball so she would be able to take a bite without getting sauce all over her chin. "Stardust and I won a couple of ribbons, and I even got a first place!" She popped the whole forkful of spaghetti into her mouth, enjoying the tangy tomato sauce that was Caroline's special recipe.

"That's great, Ash," Mr. Griffen said. "Stardust has really turned out to be a nice horse for you." He reached for the salad bowl and piled a generous helping on his plate. "I remember when we first brought her home and you had all that trouble."

Mrs. Griffen rolled her eyes and laughed. "I can't tell you how many times I came close to sending that mare back where she came from," she admitted.

Ashleigh almost choked on her pasta. "You're kidding!"

Mrs. Griffen shook her head. "It's no joke, Ash. I was really worried for a while. Stardust just didn't seem to want to behave, and I was afraid you would get hurt. But, like your father said, she's turned out to be a great horse for you."

Ashleigh nodded in agreement. She decided that now would be a good time to ask her parents' permission to show on the local circuit for the spring season. Since it was a local horse club, it would cost only eight dollars to enter each class, and she had a little extra in her savings account.

"I think I'd like to show Stardust with Mona and Frisky for the spring shows," she said. "I've got enough of my birthday money left to pay for the first couple of shows," she volunteered.

Rory wiped his sleeve across his mouth, leaving a big red mark on his shirt. "Ashleigh wants to win that new saddle," he said. "Some famous guy made it."

"I think that would be an excellent thing to work toward," Mr. Griffen agreed. "As long as you keep up with your chores, your mother and I will pay for your classes."

Caroline got up to refill the salad bowl. "Do you think you have a chance at winning the saddle?" she asked.

Ashleigh shrugged. "I did pretty well today." She tried not to sound as if she was bragging. "I did as well as Jamie, Lynne, and Mona. I think I might have as good a chance as they do at winning the prize." She didn't mention that Lisa might be a real problem once she started riding her new gelding.

"Great!" Mr. Griffen said. "Maybe we won't have to sell off a broodmare or two to buy you a new saddle," he teased.

Ashleigh laughed. "I hope our horses are worth more than that!" She finished her dinner and asked to be excused, taking her plate into the kitchen to rinse and stack in the dishwasher. She had homework to do, but first she wanted to call Mona to tell her that she'd definitely be joining her for the spring show season.

She went to the phone in the living room and dialed

her friend's number. Mona picked it up on the second ring.

"Wow, so Lisa will have two of us to worry about," Mona said when she heard Ashleigh's news.

"I can't believe how mean she was to you after Frisky bucked you off," Ashleigh said in disbelief. "That was just bad sportsmanship."

"That's all the more reason for me to beat her," Mona said. "She keeps bragging about how she's going to be the one to win the prize, but she's in for a real surprise. Now that Frisky's problem is solved, I can get down to some serious practicing. The only thing Lisa understands is winning, and *I'm* going to be the top rider at those shows."

Ashleigh frowned. If Mona was the top rider, then she'd win the prize. Ashleigh wanted Mona to be happy, but she also really wanted that saddle. If she was going to get it, she would have to compete seriously against her best friend. She just hoped that things wouldn't get too rough.

6

"She's here!" Rory hollered as he ran down the barn aisle.

Several broodmares snorted and shied when the little boy zoomed past them on his way to the barn office.

Ashleigh stepped from one of the stalls and snagged the back of Rory's shirt. "You know you're not supposed to run in the barn," she warned.

"Let go, Ash!" He squirmed to free himself. "I've got to tell Mom and Dad that Misty Flight is here."

Ashleigh quickly finished spreading the straw in Misty's stall, then ran to greet the Millers. Her parents were helping unload the new arrival when she stepped from the barn. Ashleigh felt her heartbeat quicken. The gray mare was even more beautiful in person than she was in the photos.

Misty Flight backed from the trailer and stood with her head held high as she gazed at her new surroundings. She tossed her black mane and called to the mares and foals out in the pasture. Stardust trotted up to the fence and nickered a greeting. From the other side of the barn, Royal Renegade, Edgardale's new stallion, called an invitation.

Mr. Griffen took Misty's lead and smiled as the mare answered the stallion's call with a loud whinny. "If all goes well, you'll be introduced to that handsome fellow in another month." He led the mare into the barn.

Ashleigh watched the graceful way Misty carried herself. She had a long, beautiful stride and a way about her that said she was pure class. Ashleigh studied the hoofprints she left in the dirt. She noticed Misty's back feet overstepped the front by at least six inches. Good, she thought. The mare's unimpeded stride meant she was sound and tracking straight.

Mrs. Miller handed Ashleigh an envelope. "I've brought Misty's pedigree and race records," she said. "There might be something in there that will help you figure out what her problem is. Neither Dan nor I nor the trainer has a clue as to what's gone wrong with Misty."

Ashleigh tucked the envelope under her arm. She couldn't wait to sit down with her parents and study the contents. But first they had to get Misty settled in.

Mr. Griffen turned the mare loose in her new stall. Misty circled it several times with her nose low to the ground, sniffing the deep bedding and pawing in several spots. After a few moments she found her hay net and ripped a huge mouthful from the nylon net, chewing noisily as she stared out the door at everyone gathered around.

Mr. Griffen turned to the Millers. "Let's step into the office and finish up the details. Ashleigh can keep an eye on Misty until she's settled down."

"She's very pretty," Caroline said as she stepped up to the stall door and peered in at the large gray mare.

Rory stood on his tiptoes, nodding in agreement with his older sister.

Ashleigh was surprised. Caroline never paid much attention to any of the new horses they brought in.

"Too bad she's a racehorse," Caroline said to Ashleigh. "I bet you'd win a lot of classes if you rode this mare in the show ring."

Ashleigh knew Caroline was right. This mare was even better-looking than Lisa's new Irish Thoroughbred.

Just then a bang sounded from the other end of the barn. Ashleigh grinned. It seemed that Royal Renegade didn't want to wait an entire month to meet the new mare.

Misty's head popped up at the loud noise, and she made a quick circle of her stall, then hung her head over the door and weaved from side to side, picking up each leg and shifting her weight from one to the other in a rhythmic dance.

Caroline laughed. "What's she doing? It looks like she's dancing."

"She's stall weaving," Ashleigh replied, stepping forward and shooing the mare away from the door. Misty backed quickly and stood in the center of her stall with her ears pricked and eyes rotated in the direction of the stallion. She stomped her feet and began popping her lips together in a nervous cadence.

"Wow, she can dance and provide her own beat!" Caroline chuckled. "I've never seen a horse do that before."

Ashleigh narrowed her eyes. "It looks like she's got a lot of nervous habits," she observed. "She's been on the track a long time. Some racehorses pick up really weird traits when they're cooped up in a stall for too long and fed all that hot feed." She heard a door open and turned to see her parents escorting the Millers back to their vehicle. She waved goodbye to them. "I'll take good care of her!" she called out to Mrs. Miller.

The tall, elegant lady waved back. "I know you will, Ashleigh. We'll see you soon."

When her parents returned, Ashleigh handed them the packet Mrs. Miller had given her. "That's Misty's information. Can I help you go over it? Mrs. Miller said it might give us some clues as to why Misty isn't running so well anymore."

Mr. Griffen gave a regal flourish of his hand, indicating that Ashleigh should lead the way to the office. He opened the envelope and laid the contents across the table. "Where should we start?"

Mrs. Griffen picked up Misty's pedigree chart. "I've studied this before when we first started looking at Misty, but I had forgotten just how many good horses she has in her background," she said as she glanced over the sheet. "It's no wonder the Millers want so much money for this mare. The stud fee on her sire alone was fifteen thousand dollars."

"Here's what I'm looking for," Mr. Griffen said as he pulled out the race results from the *Daily Racing Form.* "This will give us all of her racing information."

Ashleigh looked at the racing charts over her father's shoulder. "Wow, Misty brought back a paycheck every time she ran except for her last three races," she said. Ashleigh knew that most tracks paid a portion of the win purse down to fifth place. The money for fourth and fifth places often wasn't much more than the amount of the jockey fee, but Misty had a lot of firsts, seconds, and thirds on her chart.

Mrs. Griffen studied the chart. "What is it about the last three races that's different?" she asked. "Did it rain? Was the track muddy?"

Ashleigh shook her head. "One race had a fast track, one muddy, and the other dry. She did about the same in all of them."

Mr. Griffen sat back in his chair and rubbed his forehead. "I don't see anything in here that would tell us why Misty isn't running well," he said with a sigh. "She's in with the same class of horses, and she's been running in the same types of race for years now."

Mrs. Griffen stood and gathered all the papers, stuffing them back into the envelope. "I guess we're just going to have to figure this one out for ourselves," she said.

Ashleigh grabbed a handful of carrots to take to the new mare. It wouldn't hurt to make friends as soon as possible. "When does Misty start training?"

"Mike and Rhoda will be here on Wednesday to give Misty her first gallop on the Wortons' training track," Mr. Griffen said as he stood and pushed in his chair.

Rhoda was coming? Ashleigh couldn't contain her grin. Rhoda Kat was one of her favorite jockeys. She had ridden several of Ashleigh's favorite horses to victory. Ashleigh felt much better knowing that Rhoda would be riding Misty. If anyone could help the troubled mare, it was Rhoda.

"How's Frisky doing?" Ashleigh asked as she and Mona took their seats on the school bus Monday morning.

Mona brushed her short dark hair back from her face and handed Ashleigh an extra cookie she had brought with her. "My parents want me to give her a couple of days off," she said. "But I'll be ready to start back with her tomorrow. Do you want to come over and ride in the arena with me? We need to practice so we can beat Lisa."

Ashleigh shook her head. "I won't be able to ride for a few days. I've got some book reports I have to turn in, and my parents are going to show me everything I've got to do to help with Misty. Mike and Rhoda will be over on Wednesday to give Misty her first work." Ashleigh smiled. "You should see her. She's so beautiful!"

Ashleigh stared out the window at the rolling fields of Kentucky bluegrass and imagined racing across the turf on Misty's strong back, feeling the power of her long stride as the ground passed quickly beneath them.

"Earth to Ashleigh!" Mona waved her hand in front of Ashleigh's face with a laugh. "Where are you?"

Ashleigh snapped back to attention. "Sorry. I was just dreaming about riding Misty."

The bus pulled into the school parking lot, and Mona reached for their bags, handing Ashleigh hers. "You'd better worry about riding Stardust," she warned. "Lisa will be riding her new horse pretty soon, and he'll be hard to beat. How about if I bring Frisky over on Wednesday? We can ride in your front paddock, then watch Misty work."

Ashleigh jostled her way into the line of kids exiting the bus and made room for Mona. "Sounds good," she said. "I'll see you at lunch, and we'll talk more about it."

To Ashleigh's surprise, the morning passed quickly—normally when Ashleigh was in a hurry to get home to one of the horses, the school day would seem to drag on forever. When the lunch bell rang, she filed out with the rest of her class. Mona and Jamie were already at a table eating their bagged lunches. Ashleigh sat across from them. She opened her lunch bag to find a peanut butter sandwich, an apple, a bag of potato chips, and some store-bought cookies. Jamie's tuna sandwich looked much better.

"I heard Lisa is going to be riding her old gelding again in the next show," Jamie said.

Lynne plunked her lunch tray down on the table and squeezed in beside Ashleigh.

"But what happens when she switches horses?" Ashleigh asked. "What will happen to any points she wins?"

Lynne traded her bologna sandwich for Ashleigh's peanut butter, but she refused to swap her homemade apple pie for the dry cookies. "The points follow the rider, not the horse," she explained. "You're allowed to use different horses, but only one horse per show."

Ashleigh nodded as she inspected the bologna sandwich, lifting the slices of bread so she could put a layer of potato chips in the sandwich. "Too bad I didn't have another horse to ride," she said. "That would be cool if you could pick your best horse."

Mona watched Ashleigh layer the potato chips onto the bologna sandwich. "Talk about gross!"

Ashleigh smushed the bread together and handed the sandwich to her friend. "Try it. It's really good."

Mona made a face, but she took a small bite, crunching the potato chips as she chewed. Her eyebrows rose. "Mmm, that's a lot better than it looks. Want to trade for a ham sandwich?"

"No way!" She took her sandwich back before Mona could make the switch.

They spent the rest of the lunch hour talking about the upcoming show. Most of the conversation was about how badly Mona wanted to beat Lisa. Ashleigh kept quiet and finished her lunch. Each of her friends owned a registered Thoroughbred. Stardust had held her own against them in the first show, where no points had been awarded, but Jamie and Lynne weren't in all the classes she had entered. She took a bite of one of the dry cookies, then tossed the rest of them into the bag. Mona was right. If she was going to compete in these shows, she'd really need to start practicing.

The five-minute warning bell rang. Ashleigh packed up the rest of her lunch and stood to leave.

Jamie waved goodbye. "We'll see you at the show this weekend, right?"

Ashleigh nodded. She owed it to herself and her old saddle to give it at least one more try before she decided it wasn't worth the effort.

Wednesday finally arrived. Ashleigh had both Stardust and Misty brushed and ready. She was just saddling her mare when Mona rode up on Frisky. "I'll be out in a minute," she called out the barn door. "Go ahead and warm up in the front paddock. I'll be there as soon as I get my tack on."

She snugged the girth and pulled the bridle over Stardust's ears, then walked the mare from the barn. Mona was trotting Frisky in circles. The bay mare was bobbing her head up and down as she trotted.

"Did you check that bit, too?" Ashleigh asked as she led Stardust to the mounting block and slipped into the old saddle.

Mona wiggled her reins, trying to get Frisky to give at the poll and quit tossing her head. "I checked all my bits and looked at the inside of Frisky's mouth," she said. "There wasn't any problem. I don't know why she's doing this."

Ashleigh guided Stardust to the gate and bent to open the latch. She took the mare through the opening, then closed the gate behind them. "Maybe Frisky just wants some company." She rode up beside the bay, and they circled the arena at a walk and then a trot. Frisky leaned in on Stardust as they made another circle.

"I hope she doesn't do that in the show," Ashleigh said.

They worked for another half hour, and Frisky continued to make little mistakes. Stardust was going well and taking all the cues that Ashleigh gave her. They were working on lead changes when Rhoda and Mike pulled into the stable yard. Rhoda hopped out of her little red sports car and waved.

"Let's put the mares in a stall and go talk to Rhoda while Mike saddles Misty." Ashleigh turned Stardust toward the gate. "Maybe she'll let us ride over to the Wortons' with her."

It had been a while since Ashleigh had last seen the petite, dark-haired jockey, and she was excited to talk to her. Ashleigh listened eagerly to Rhoda's stories about wild horses and big races while they waited for Mike to finish tacking Misty.

A moment later the stocky trainer led Misty from her stall and nodded to Ashleigh. "Good to see you again, kiddo." He walked Misty from the barn and gave Rhoda a leg up.

Ashleigh and Mona quickly ran to get their mounts. "Can I pony you over to the Wortons'?" she asked.

Rhoda waved both girls over. "You can ride with me if you want, but this mare is so gentle, I don't need a pony."

Ashleigh raised her eyebrows. "She's seemed kind of excitable the last couple of days," she said.

Rhoda bent her knee outward and reached down to pull the girth another notch tighter as they rode down the path to the neighbor's farm. "Don't let this big lug fool you," she said with a chuckle. "She's just settling in and getting used to the place. She's so gentle, you could probably ride her yourself, Ash."

Ashleigh grinned. If only Rhoda knew how many times over the past few days she'd dreamed about doing exactly that!

Mona rode up next to Ashleigh. "I guess Frisky finally decided she was worn out," Mona said. "Look at her now. She's behaving perfectly."

Ashleigh's brow furrowed as she thought about the

bay mare's behavior. Frisky had always been a reliable, steady horse. Why was she suddenly moving from one extreme to the other? One thing was for sure—if they didn't figure out the answer quickly, Mona would fall behind in show points, and it would be up to Ashleigh to make sure that Lisa didn't win the saddle. But what if she and Stardust weren't up to the task?

7

They arrived at the Wortons' property, then circled around the half-mile training track to the barn area on the other side, where Mike and Mr. Griffen were waiting.

"Good afternoon," Dan Worton called as he walked to meet them. His wife, Jane, waved from where she stood, hosing off a young Thoroughbred. Mr. Worton nodded to indicate an empty pen. "You girls can put your mares in there for now. We'll see you out at the track in a moment."

"Thanks, Mr. Worton," Ashleigh said as she dismounted and led Stardust to the corral. They removed the bridles from both the horses but left the saddles on. Ashleigh hoped that Stardust wouldn't roll, but she figured it couldn't damage the saddle any more than it already was.

"Let's hurry," Mona said as she ducked through the gate. "Misty's already stepping onto the track."

Mike was calling directions to Rhoda when Ashleigh and Mona joined the rest of the small group.

"Take her for two slow rounds," Mike instructed. "I just want to see how she goes—nothing fancy." He ran a hand through his graying hair and leaned on the rail.

Ashleigh crowded in next to Mike, her eyes never leaving Rhoda and Misty. She watched as the young jockey backtracked the mare clockwise around the track for several hundred yards. When they turned to go counterclockwise, Rhoda made the big gray halt and face the inner rail for several moments before asking her to move on.

Ashleigh knew that the reason jockeys asked the horses to stop was so that the animals wouldn't get into the habit of making the turn and charging right into a gallop. But Misty didn't seem to be in any hurry. She took her time, walking for several feet before breaking into a slow trot at Rhoda's cue. The mare ambled along, turning her head to observe everything going on around her. Rhoda had to cluck several times before she could get Misty to go into a slow, plodding canter.

"Isn't she supposed to have a little more oomph than that?" Mona asked. "She looks like the most easygoing racehorse I've ever seen."

Mike kept his eye on the mare as she slowly circled the training track. "I don't think it's anything to worry about. This whole place is new to Misty, and she's just having a look around. Her mind doesn't seem to be on racing at the moment."

Ashleigh wondered if that was an understatement. Misty stared at everything around the outside of the track as she puttered along at a hobbyhorse canter. On the second time around, the big gray switched leads many times and lugged toward the outside of the race-track.

"Why is she doing that?" Ashleigh asked.

Mr. Griffen shaded his eyes so he could watch the mare go into the upper turn. "That looks pretty unusual to me," he said.

Mike stood silent for several moments, studying the gray mare. "There's two main reasons I can think of for that kind of behavior," he said. "Misty could have leg trouble, and when she starts hurting, she switches leads so all the pressure doesn't stay on the bad leg. But I didn't see any leg problems when I checked her over. I'll go over her more thoroughly when we get her cooled out."

"What's the other possibility?" Ashleigh asked.

Mike crossed his arms over his chest. "Some horses start playing around like that when they're bored, but this is Misty's first time on this track, and she seems to be taking in everything. I don't think that could be it."

Misty slowly circled the course. When she came past them this time, Rhoda sat down in the saddle, and Misty immediately made for the outside of the track, stopping and turning in to face the inner rail as if she had done the routine a million times and knew it by heart. She stepped off the track popping her lips the way she had in the stall.

Ashleigh laughed. "Why does she do that?"

Rhoda reached down under her leg to loosen the girth a notch. "Some horses pick up odd behaviors at the track," she said as she untied the knot in her reins. "I think this is just one of the strange habits she picked up to entertain herself."

Mr. Worton offered them the use of his wash rack, but Mike declined. "I don't think she got hot enough to need a bath. Rhoda can ride her back to Edgardale with the girls to cool her out, and we'll take care of her over there." He nodded for Derek Griffen to follow him to the car. "Thanks for letting us use your track, Dan and Jane. We'll be back in a few days."

Ashleigh and Mona ran to get their horses. They quickly bridled the mares and checked the saddles, then mounted up and followed Rhoda back to Edgar-dale.

"What do you think?" Ashleigh asked the jockey as they walked down the trail.

Rhoda shrugged. "I'm not sure," she admitted. "Misty doesn't seem to have any fire left."

Mona trotted Frisky up closer to Rhoda so that she could hear what the jockey had to say. "Maybe she's just tired from the move," she suggested.

"I guess," Rhoda said. "We'll be back on Friday to gallop her again. She'll have a few days to get rested up, so we'll see how she does then."

They rode into Edgardale's stable yard. Jonas came out to hold Misty so that Rhoda could dismount and pull her tack. Ashleigh said goodbye to Mona, then quickly untacked Stardust and put her in a stall so she could help with Misty.

"You don't mind waiting here a few minutes until I can get back to brush you, do you, girl?" Ashleigh said to Stardust as she tossed the mare a flake of hay to keep her occupied. Stardust wasn't hot or sweaty, so Ashleigh knew she'd be fine while she helped with the racehorse.

Rhoda waved to Ashleigh on the way to her car. "I'll see you on Friday."

Ashleigh smiled and returned the wave, then went to help her father and Mike with Misty. They were discussing the workout when she arrived.

Mike shook his head. "I want to see her go another time or two before I make you a workout schedule, Derek," the trainer said as he ran a stiff brush over the small sweaty areas where the saddle had been. "Misty'll be more comfortable with her surroundings by Friday, and we may get an entirely different type of work out of her." He handed the mare's lead rope to Ashleigh. "You can put her back in her stall now. If you want, you can open up the back door so she can go out into the run during the daytime."

Ashleigh led the mare back to her stall. She grabbed a couple of carrots and fed them to Misty. The mare wiggled her lips and begged for the treat. When Ashleigh was a little slow with the last carrot, Misty bobbed her head and popped her lips together. The sound made Ashleigh laugh.

"Don't spoil that horse too much," Mike warned as he poked his head into the barn. "I'll be back to see you again on Friday. We'll try the same routine," he said.

Ashleigh nodded and waved goodbye. She felt a soft muzzle poke at her shoulder and turned to see Misty staring at her. "Sorry," she said as she turned her palms upward to show she didn't have any more treats. "The carrots are all gone."

Misty blew through her lips, then hung her head over the door and began to weave as she shifted her weight from one leg to the other in a strange dance.

"Stop that!" Ashleigh said. "That's not good for your legs. Mike says you're sound now, but if you keep doing that, your legs might get sore." She ducked into the stall and opened the back doors into the twenty-foot run. Misty pricked her ears and walked out into the sunshine. She walked the fence line several times and then stood staring at the pasture that held the broodmares and weanlings.

Ashleigh watched the mare for a few moments. Something was bothering Misty, and she couldn't figure out what. Maybe the workout on Friday would shed some light on why the mare had taken the sudden turn in attitude.

On the way home from school on Friday, Ashleigh invited Mona over to ride to the Wortons' with her and Rhoda.

Mona picked up her backpack, which was already so full, it looked ready to split. "I can't," she said as she jammed her social studies book in next to her math book. "I've got a lesson with my trainer. Frisky has been horrible these last two days."

"But she was doing fine when we were riding with Rhoda," Ashleigh said, surprised. "What's she doing now?"

Mona flopped back into the seat and breathed an

exasperated sigh. "She's doing everything wrong."

Ashleigh frowned. "What does your trainer say you should do?"

"Theresa thinks I'm being too easy on Frisky," Mona said as she brushed her dark hair behind her ears and stared out the bus window. "She says I can't let Frisky get away with being a brat. She wants me to come for more lessons."

The bus slowed for their stop, and Ashleigh stood up. "I hope you get everything worked out today. The show is tomorrow, and all of the points count in this one."

"I know," Mona said with a worried look. "I've got just twenty-four hours to find the cure for Frisky. We've got to win some classes tomorrow so Lisa doesn't get ahead on the points."

Mrs. Cecil smiled and said goodbye as they stepped from the bus.

"I have to get Stardust ready to go with Rhoda," Ashleigh said. "That looks like her car in the driveway. I'll see you tomorrow morning for the show." She waved to Mona, then turned and jogged down Edgardale's long drive.

Mrs. Griffen handed Ashleigh her helmet when she walked into the barn. "Stardust is already tacked," she said. "Rhoda and Mike are ready to go."

Ashleigh pulled Stardust from her stall and checked

her tack, then led her outside to mount up. Rhoda and Misty were right behind her. They took a moment to let the mares sniff noses and then set off down the trail to the Wortons' farm.

Misty seemed to have a little more spunk than before, and Ashleigh hoped that she would show more interest in her workout, but when Rhoda guided the mare onto the track, the big gray dragged her feet at a walk and broke into the same sluggish canter she had used on Wednesday.

"Open her up a little down the backside," Mike hollered to Rhoda when she cantered past.

Ashleigh leaned on the rail and kept her fingers crossed. Thoroughbreds loved to run. Misty was probably just waiting for the chance to show off.

But Ashleigh and the others were disappointed again. Misty lengthened her stride, but she continued to fuss and lugged heavily to the outside rail.

Mike ran a hand through his short hair. "I don't know what to tell you, Derek. I think maybe we need to give Misty some company so she'll keep her mind on the business at hand. I'll arrange to have one of the Wortons' horses work with us on Sunday. Maybe that'll bring her interest back."

Ashleigh glanced at Rhoda as she walked the big horse off the track. She could tell by the doubtful look on the jockey's face that Rhoda was beginning to worry. If Rhoda was worried, then Ashleigh was, too. If Misty didn't win this next race, the Millers wouldn't have the extra purse money, and Misty wouldn't be coming to Edgardale to live.

The big race was only weeks away. If they didn't solve Misty's problem soon, it would be too late.

8

Ashleigh checked her show equipment for the hundredth time. She glanced at the clock on the barn wall. Where was Mona? Her friend should have been there a half hour earlier. She went to the phone to try the Gardners' house again, but no one answered.

Stardust stood with her head hanging over the door, watching curiously as Misty Flight weaved back and forth in her doorway and popped her lips.

"Why do you do that?" Ashleigh said as she took the mare's head between her hands to stop the back-and-forth motion. Misty nibbled on the front of her shirt and checked her pockets for carrots. "Sorry, I don't have any with me," Ashleigh said. She let herself into Misty's stall and opened the back door so the mare could go out into her run.

Misty stepped into the sunshine and made a loop of

her pen before stopping in the corner and dropping her head to doze in the warm sunshine. Ashleigh was relieved that the gray was taking a break from her weird habits.

A horn blasted from the stable yard, and Ashleigh ran to get Stardust and her show tack. "What happened?" she asked as she handed Stardust to Mona to load while she put her equipment in the tack compartment.

Mona led Stardust to the trailer and tossed the rope over the mare's neck, stepping aside as the little chestnut loaded by herself. "Frisky refused to get in the trailer this morning," Mona said with a frown. "My dad had to come out and help us. It took a half hour to convince her to get into the trailer."

Ashleigh hooked the butt strap behind Stardust so that she couldn't back out, then closed the trailer door. "Did something in the trailer spook her?"

Mona slid into the front seat of the pickup next to her mother and waited for Ashleigh to get in. "I didn't see or hear anything, but I guess that's possible." She let out a heavy sigh. "I just don't know what's going on with Frisky. I've been working so hard with her, and none of it seems to be sinking in. She'd better behave at the show today. I don't want to be embarrassed like I was last week."

Ashleigh buckled her seatbelt, and the truck pulled

out of the yard. "It'll work out," she said with confidence. "This is going to be a great show for both of us. We're going to get some points for the saddle!"

Mona smiled weakly. They rode in silence for the rest of the short drive to the arena.

"Oh, no," Mrs. Gardner said when they pulled onto the show grounds. "It doesn't look like there are any parking places left."

Ashleigh stared out over the rows of horse trailers. She couldn't see an empty spot anywhere. "Maybe we'll have to park in the back lot near where they park the regular cars."

Mona cringed. "That would be horrible! It's so far from everyone else. We won't even be able to hear the gate calls from over there."

Mrs. Gardner turned the truck down the road that led to the backside of the arena. "It looks like we don't have any choice, girls. The parking lot is full, and I don't want to get this trailer stuck in some tiny spot where there's no room to turn around."

Mona leaned back in the seat and frowned. "Things haven't gone right since I got out of bed," she said in a defeated tone. "I've got a really bad feeling about this show."

Mrs. Gardner pulled the truck to a halt in an area with lots of space. Two more trailers pulled in behind them. Ashleigh jumped from the truck and went to unload the mares. "We'd better hurry," she said. "We're really late, and it won't be long before they call the first class."

"I'll tack the horses while you girls go get your numbers," Mrs. Gardner volunteered.

"Thanks, Mom," Mona said as she motioned for Ashleigh to follow her.

Ashleigh winced as they cut across the big dirt parking lot. English riding boots weren't made for running. She'd be lucky if she didn't have blisters by the time they got back to the trailer. They reached the show office and got their packets with their numbers and classes.

"Look!" Ashleigh pointed to the corner of the room, where the prize saddle sat on a portable saddle rack. "There it is! I'm going to sit in it and see if it fits."

Mona peered around to see if anyone was looking. "I don't know if you should, Ash."

Ashleigh ignored her. "It will just take a second," she said, and climbed into the Robbie Ward saddle. It was a perfect fit.

A loud snicker came from the doorway. Lisa Martin poked her head into the room. "Don't get too comfortable in that saddle," she said in a confident tone. "It's going to be coming home with me." She ducked from the room, laughing as she walked away.

Ashleigh climbed down from the saddle. She stood there for a moment, unable to even speak.

Mona glared after Lisa. "I really don't like that girl." She walked over to the saddle and ran her hand across the expensive brown leather. "Lisa won't laugh so hard when this saddle goes home with me."

Ashleigh hesitated. "But what if I win the saddle?" she asked. Mona's eyebrows shot up in shock, and it was as if it had never occurred to her friend that Ashleigh had just as good a chance to win as she did.

Mona frowned. "I've got to win this saddle, Ash. That's the only thing that will make Lisa leave me alone."

Ashleigh didn't know what to say, so she kept quiet and followed Mona back to the horse trailer.

Mrs. Gardner had the horses ready by the time they returned. "If you listen really hard, you can barely hear them call the classes. The walk-trot class starts in ten minutes. You girls had better get your helmets on and get in those saddles." She took a rag and polished the dirt off their boots once they were mounted. "Good luck!" she called as Ashleigh and Mona trotted across the lot toward the arena.

Frisky tossed her head and pricked her ears toward all the activity by the arena. Mona leaned down to pat her on the neck. "Don't let me down, girl," she whispered.

Their class was just passing into the arena when they arrived at the gate. Ashleigh waved to Jamie. "Where's Lynne?" she asked.

Jamie reined her horse in behind Ashleigh, waiting for her turn to pass through the gate. "She woke up with a nasty cold, and her parents wouldn't let her come. That'll probably put her out of the running for the saddle."

"Let's go, girls," the ring steward called as he checked off their numbers and motioned them forward.

Ashleigh concentrated on keeping Stardust collected into a nice trot. She glanced at Mona, who was several horses ahead of her. Frisky seemed to be behaving well, and Ashleigh noticed that the judge kept her eye on the pair for several moments longer than he did the others. The judge called for a walk and then a reverse of direction. Before long the horses were called into the center of the ring to line up. The judge came to each horse in turn and asked for a backup. Stardust and Frisky executed the drill well, but several of the horses ran into the horse next to them.

When the winners were called, Mona took the first-place ribbon and Ashleigh got second. A girl from their school named Peggy took third, and Jamie got fourth. Lisa sulked as she trotted up to receive her fifth-place ribbon.

Ashleigh and Mona both placed in their next two classes. But by the time the English equitation class rolled around, Frisky was misbehaving. Ashleigh won that class, and Lisa placed fourth, but Mona spent the entire time fighting with Frisky and didn't even get a ribbon.

"She's doing it again," Mona said in dismay as they waited for their next class. "How can she win one class and place dead last in another?"

"We only have a few more classes left," Ashleigh said. "If Frisky can hold it together and get through the next couple of classes, you'll be fine. You guys placed well in most of your other rounds."

But when the call came for their next class, Frisky balked at the gate, refusing to enter the ring.

"Come on, girl," Mona pleaded as she used her legs to propel the mare forward. But Frisky wouldn't budge. Mona turned the mare in a tight circle and asked for forward motion again, but Frisky refused to enter the ring. "I think she's spooking at that guy in the white shirt standing next to the fence," Mona said with a frown.

But to Ashleigh it seemed as though Frisky was just being obstinate. Frisky didn't even appear to be looking at the man in the white shirt.

Mona tried once more, but Frisky refused to pass through the gate. "I'm going to sit out the rest of my classes until the jump class," she told Ashleigh, then turned from the gate and headed back toward the trailer with her shoulders slumped.

Ashleigh had a difficult time listening to the judge's

calls in her next two classes—she kept thinking about Mona and Frisky and what had gone wrong. She was pleasantly surprised to find that she won the equitation class and placed third behind Lisa for the English pleasure class.

Mona congratulated Ashleigh when they met for a quick lunch break back at the trailer, but Ashleigh could hear the underlying sadness in her friend's voice.

"I've got this figured out," Mona said as she grabbed a tuna sandwich from the cooler. "You, me, Lisa, Jamie, and Peggy are all close in the point spread. The green-hunter-over-fences class will determine who gets the most points for the day."

Ashleigh sipped her soda. "You're going to ride Frisky in the class?"

"Of course," Mona said. "I have to do well in this class to edge out Lisa. Let's finish our lunch and get back over there. The ring will stay open for practice jumps until ten minutes before the class starts."

They quickly finished their lunches and rode back to the arena. They cantered around the arena several times to warm up, and then Ashleigh made a pass at the jumps. Stardust sailed over the low hurdles without any faults, but Frisky balked on her first try. Mona bumped the mare hard with her heels, and Ashleigh looked around to see if any of the judges or stewards were watching. She didn't want to see Mona get disqualified for misusing her horse.

Mona made another attempt at the jump, and this time Frisky sailed over the rails.

"Let's call it quits until the class," Ashleigh suggested.

Mona nodded and followed her out of the arena. They stood along the rail and waited for the class to be called. Ashleigh cringed when she saw Lisa ride up on Rusty.

"Nice refusal on that first jump," Lisa said in a catty tone. "If she does that during the class, you'll be out of the running today."

Ashleigh turned in her saddle to face Lisa. "Why don't you leave us alone?" she said. "Frisky can outjump Rusty any day of the week, and you know it!"

The horses were called to enter the ring. Lisa looked at them and scoffed. "I guess we'll find out now, won't we?" she said arrogantly as she trotted into the ring.

Mona looked ready to cry. Ashleigh was so mad, she could feel her hands shaking on the reins. The tension caused Stardust to toss her head and root at the bit. "Sorry, girl," she said as she tried to calm down. But she couldn't get Lisa's words out of her head. "Don't pay any attention to her," Ashleigh said to Mona. "She's just a brat, and she's trying to psych you out so she can beat you and Frisky."

"But she *will* beat us if Frisky keeps acting up," Mona insisted.

The ring steward waved them into the arena. Ashleigh turned to Mona. "Don't talk like that," she said. "You and Frisky are going to win this class!" She trotted Stardust into the ring and breathed a sigh of relief when she saw Frisky right behind them.

Ashleigh was still shaking when her turn came. She tried to steady her hands and guide Stardust over the jumps, but the little mare was unsure of her rider's signals and took off too soon on the last jump. Ashleigh grimaced as she heard the horse's hooves knock the pole to the ground. She trotted Stardust over to stand with the others, ignoring Lisa's I-told-you-so smile.

Lisa was the next to go. Rusty cleared the jumps, but he wasn't a pretty jumper. The chestnut gelding ran too close to the jump and then popped straight over, landing with a jolt on the other side. But Lisa must have thought he did well, because she joined them with a triumphant smile.

Mona and Frisky were the last to go. Ashleigh crossed her fingers as Mona circled Frisky at a slow canter and then pointed her toward the first jump. Frisky's ears flicked back and forth, and Ashleigh could see Mona putting more leg on the mare to keep her moving forward. Suddenly Frisky's ears pricked toward the jump.

Ashleigh held her breath. Had Frisky seen something that drew her attention and was going to make her spook, or would she sail over the jump like a champion?

9

Ashleigh smiled in relief as Frisky sailed over the jumps, making a perfect round. She traded grins with Mona as she trotted back to join the rest of the competitors. Everyone knew that Mona had won the class.

Mona smiled proudly as she went forward to claim her first-place ribbon. Ashleigh knew her own performance wasn't enough to garner a ribbon. She waited patiently while all the places were called, resisting the urge to poke fun at a frazzled Lisa, who sat beside her gritting her teeth as she watched Mona ride from the ring with the blue ribbon.

"I can't believe I got the high point score for the day!" Mona said later as they made the turn into Edgardale's driveway. "And you're in third place, Ash!"

Ashleigh smiled. She had to admit she was doing

better than she'd thought she might. She was still within reach of winning that awesome saddle.

The truck pulled up in front of Edgardale's large brown barn, and Mr. and Mrs. Griffen came out to help unload Stardust and carry in the tack. "I'd say by the smiles on your faces that you two must have done pretty well," Mr. Griffen observed.

Ashleigh nodded as she opened the trailer door and asked Stardust to back out. "Mona had the most points for the day, and I'm in third place," she said, pointing to the ribbons that hung from her bridle. A welcoming neigh caught her attention, and Ashleigh turned to see Misty Flight jogging around the front paddock.

"We decided to let Misty out to stretch her legs," Mrs. Griffen said as she gathered Ashleigh's tack and headed for the barn. "She really seems to be enjoying herself out there."

Ashleigh turned to Mona. "Do you want to come over tomorrow to watch Misty work?" she asked. "Rhoda is going to work her with one of the Wortons' horses. It should be fun."

Mona shook her head. "I can't, Ash. Frisky and I are in first place now, and I can't afford to let up. We've got to work extra to fix Frisky's problems so that I don't blow any more classes." She stepped into the truck and waved goodbye. "I'll see you in school on Monday."

Ashleigh frowned as she watched the Gardners' truck pull away. Her heart felt heavy. In her drive to beat Lisa, Mona seemed to be forgetting about everything else.

The following morning Ashleigh was up early, helping Jonas with the feed and making sure that Misty would be ready when Mike and Rhoda arrived. She dumped the grain into the mare's bucket and watched as Misty shoved her muzzle deep into the oat-and-sweet-feed concoction. "You're going to do well today," she said as she patted the mare's sleek neck, admiring the way the dark dapples accented her lighter gray coat.

Misty finished the grain and nickered greedily for her hay.

"Sorry, girl," Ashleigh apologized. "You're going to be breezing today, so you can't have any hay until you get home." She slipped the mare a small bite of Stardust's grass hay. "We don't want you feeling weighed down. You've got to beat that colt the Wortons are sending against you."

Ashleigh busied herself cleaning stalls until Mike and Rhoda arrived. As soon as she heard the little red sports car roar into the driveway, she pulled Misty from the stall and helped her father put on the exercise saddle and bridle.

"Good morning," Rhoda said as she stepped into the barn. Her dark hair was pulled back in a long braid, and her black leather exercise boots shone from a good polishing.

"I think she's ready to get down to some serious work this morning," Mr. Griffen said as he led Misty from the barn and waited for Mike to give Rhoda a leg up.

Rhoda knotted her reins and checked the length of her irons. She looked up in surprise when Ashleigh walked to the pickup with Mike and Mr. Griffen. "Aren't you riding with me today?"

Ashleigh shook her head. "Stardust worked hard at the show yesterday. She won a bunch of ribbons, so I decided to treat her to a day off in the pasture."

"That's great, Ash," the petite jockey said. "Congratulations! I didn't even know you were showing this year."

Ashleigh shrugged. "I hadn't planned on it, but they're giving away a Ward saddle as a prize, and I need a new saddle really badly."

Rhoda buckled her chin strap and smiled knowingly. "Especially *that* new saddle. I'll keep my fingers crossed for you." She waved. "I'll see you guys at the track."

They drove to the Wortons' farm, and Ashleigh

watched one of the grooms tack the young gelding that would be breezing with Misty. The colt snorted and pawed at the ground as he was being saddled. He would be good competition for Misty—if she decided to rise to the challenge.

"Rhoda's here," Mike shouted from outside the barn. "Bring the colt out. We'll meet you on the track."

Ashleigh followed the Wortons' horse to the track. Misty's ears pricked in interest when the young horse entered through the gap.

Mike took his place on the rail. "Take them around easy one time, and then breeze them for the last half mile," he called to the riders.

On the first lap Misty played with her bit and tossed her head. She switched leads a couple of times, but nothing like she had been doing the previous week. The second time around, Rhoda asked the mare to pick up speed as they approached the half-mile pole. At the red-and-white-striped pole, the gelding shot into the lead.

"Come on, Misty, you can beat that horse!" Ashleigh yelled, but the gray mare hung just off the bay's haunches, lumbering to keep up with him, showing no desire to pass the gelding. They crossed the finish line with the gelding at least a length ahead of Misty.

Everyone was quiet as the horses stepped from the track.

"We'll meet you back at Edgardale," Mike said as they all walked back to the pickup. He didn't speak again until they were hosing Misty off at the wash rack.

"Well, what do you think, Mike?" Mr. Griffen asked. "Is it a hopeless cause?"

Mike scratched the gray stubble on his chin. "I think this mare is bored to death with racing," he said.

Ashleigh was shocked. "Really?"

Mike turned off the hose and used the sweat scraper to remove the excess water from Misty's body. "Misty is eight years old, and she's been racing since she was three," he explained. "A lot of mares get retired to broodmare status before that. I think she's just lost interest."

Ashleigh watched the steam rise from Misty's body in the cool morning. She handed Mike a blanket to cover the mare. "So what can we do with her?" she asked. "Misty's race is only a month away. She's got to win this race, or she doesn't get to come live at Edgardale."

Mike blanketed the mare and handed her lead rope to Ashleigh, signaling for her to walk her cool. "I think she could use a few days out in the pasture. Then we can start her back with a little light riding—maybe take her down the trails."

Ashleigh turned to Rhoda. "Will you be coming out

to go trail riding with me and Stardust?" she asked hopefully.

Rhoda shook her head. "This mare is gentle enough for you to take her on the trails, Ash. If you're worried, just have your friend pony you until you feel comfortable." She grinned. "As lazy as Misty has been, I don't think you'll have to worry about her running away." She waved goodbye and headed to her car.

Derek Griffen flashed a concerned frown. "Do you really think we should let Ashleigh ride her?" he asked.

Mike slapped him on the back good-naturedly. "That girl's going to be a great jockey someday, Derek. She might as well get some experience on this gentle old mare. Just be certain you call the Millers to make sure it's okay. Let's give Misty a few days to laze around in the pasture, and Ash can take her out for a short ride on Wednesday. If the mare's doing well, keep her going every other day, and try to work in some long, slow distances with her."

Mr. Griffen nodded as he took notes.

Ashleigh was so excited, she couldn't wait to call Mona. But first Misty had to be cooled out. She circled the barn several times, letting Misty have a look at the pasture that would be her home for the next several days. "It's right next to the babies," she said. "You'll like that."

As soon as the big gray was completely cooled out,

Ashleigh turned her into her stall and tossed her a flake of grass hay. She checked to make sure Misty's saddle and bridle were put away, and then she went to the phone to call Mona.

"Wow," Mona said when Ashleigh told her the news. "That would be so awesome to get to ride Misty. You're really lucky."

"I can't ride her by myself yet," Ashleigh said. "That's why I'm calling you. Do you think you could pony me on Wednesday?"

Mona hesitated. "I'm sorry, Ash," she apologized. "But I've got another lesson on Wednesday. I can't miss it."

Ashleigh rolled her eyes. All her friend did anymore was go to lessons. "Why can't you miss it?"

There was a long pause on the line. Finally Mona answered, "You know why I can't miss it, Ash. I can't let Lisa get ahead of me."

Ashleigh twisted the phone cord while she decided whether to keep quiet or say something about Mona's new obsession with beating Lisa. But she was at the boiling point and couldn't keep this inside much longer. "That's all you ever think about anymore," she blurted out. "There are more important things than beating Lisa. What about our friendship?" she challenged. "It's been put on hold while you worry about Lisa, and it's not fair!"

There was another long silence. After a while, her friend's stiff-sounding voice came over the phone.

"I'll be there on Wednesday after school," Mona said, then she hung up the phone.

Ashleigh placed the receiver back on its hook. Had she gone too far? Was she wrong to remind Mona that she was slipping in the friendship department?

During the next couple of days Mona wasn't herself around Ashleigh. She remained quiet and standoffish. Ashleigh wondered if she should apologize, but why should she when Mona was the one who was putting competition ahead of their friendship?

By the time Wednesday rolled around, Mona was acting more like herself. She arrived at Edgardale just as Ashleigh's parents were saddling Misty.

"I'll be right out," Ashleigh called to Mona. She put on her helmet and waited for her mother to lead Misty from the barn. "We've got to start out in the front paddock," Ashleigh said. "My parents want to make sure Misty is going to behave before we take her out on the trail."

Mr. Griffen boosted Ashleigh into the saddle and held Misty while his daughter adjusted her equipment. Then he handed them off to Mona and Frisky. "I want to watch you girls make a couple of laps out front before you take off on your own," he said.

Frisky pinned her ears at Misty when Mr. Griffen

handed Mona the lead rope. Mona gave her a warning bump and leaned over to take the gray mare.

Ashleigh felt her hands shake. Not only was Misty new to her, but she was a tall mare, and Ashleigh was far off the ground. She gulped hard and tried to steady her breathing.

"Are you okay, Ash?" Mona asked, running the pony strap through the ring on Misty's bit. "You look really pale."

Ashleigh nodded. "I'm fine. I'm just not used to being on a horse this big." She concentrated as they made several circles at a walk and then broke into a trot. Misty behaved perfectly.

"Bring her out," Mr. Griffen said. "I think you girls will be safe out on the trail with this horse. Just keep the pony strap on for today's ride in case you have any trouble."

Ashleigh nodded eagerly. "We'll be careful."

They headed toward the back fields. The trail there was wide enough for the horses to walk shoulder to shoulder. Misty covered the ground in long, sweeping strides. Frisky had to really stretch to keep up with her.

Mona let out the pony strap a bit, giving Ashleigh and Misty more room. "She's behaving really well, Ash," Mona observed. "I bet we won't have to keep this pony strap on for very long."

Ashleigh took a deep breath and loosened her reins

a little. "You're right, she is going well." Ashleigh studied Mona and Frisky. "You know, Frisky is minding better than she has in a while."

Mona sighed. "You wouldn't be saying that if you'd seen her when I was putting the saddle on. She was really grouchy, and she even tried to reach around and nip me when I pulled the girth snug."

Ashleigh remembered what Mike had said about Misty. "What if Frisky's problem is that she's bored with the show ring?" she suggested. "Maybe that's why she keeps acting out."

"That's crazy," Mona said firmly. "We go to different arenas all the time. How could she be bored?"

"But, Mona," Ashleigh argued, "you do the exact same things *all the time*! You side-pass, do flying lead changes, walk, trot, canter . . . you hardly ever go out on the trails anymore. And look," she said with a wave of her hand, indicating Frisky's calm demeanor, "Frisky's happy out here. Every time you've had her on the trail, she behaves. Maybe you should give her a week off from the arena and do more trail riding."

Mona's eyes widened in shock. "A week off?" She frowned. "That would be just what you need, right?" She blinked. "I mean, just what *Lisa* would need."

Ashleigh tilted her head. "What do you mean?" she asked, confused. She tried to steady Misty, who was getting edgy because of the raised voices.

"If Frisky and I took a week off, Lisa would pull ahead of me and have a good chance of moving into first place. Then I'd have to listen to her bragging the rest of the school year."

Ashleigh knew her friend was worried about the competition from Lisa, but she couldn't help wondering about the mistake Mona had made when she'd first said it would be best for Ashleigh, not Lisa. "I'm just trying to tell you that I think Frisky is acting up because you're doing too much of the same thing with her and she's bored with it. That's why she misbehaves. Think about it," she said. "Frisky always does well in the early classes, and she starts acting up about the time of your fourth class. When she won the jumping competition at the last show, it was because you didn't go to several of the classes before it, and we both know Frisky loves to jump."

"Well, I'm *not* taking a week off," Mona said.

Ashleigh bit her bottom lip. This was not going well. "Look, Mona," she said with a sigh, "I'm not trying to let anyone get ahead of you in the standings by playing tricks. I'm only trying to help. If Frisky keeps acting up in the ring, you won't get any points anyway, so wouldn't you be better off giving her a vacation now so that you could do really well in the last few shows?"

Ashleigh could tell by the set of her friend's jaw that Mona wasn't going to budge on this.

"I don't want to talk about this anymore," Mona said. "Let's just finish this ride and get home."

Ashleigh nodded in agreement, but her heart sank. Frisky wasn't the only one with a problem. Ashleigh had a feeling that her friendship with Mona was in big trouble, too.

10

Ashleigh and Mona sat together at lunch on Thursday afternoon, but to Ashleigh, it just wasn't the same. They were still talking, but it felt as though a wall had gone up between them. Ashleigh couldn't stop feeling hurt that Mona had really wondered if Ashleigh had her best interests in mind. And the worst part was that Lisa was sitting at the next table and hadn't stopped going on and on about herself the whole lunch period.

"I'll be riding Ranger at the next show," Lisa bragged, her voice getting even louder. "My Irish Thoroughbred will beat all those other horses." She looked pointedly at Ashleigh and Mona. "Especially those little mixed-breed things, and this one horse whose rider can't make it behave." She rubbed her hands together. "That saddle's as good as mine right now."

Ashleigh tossed the apple she was eating back into

her lunch bag. Her appetite was totally gone. Lisa was probably right. There was no way Stardust could compete with that beautiful Irish Thoroughbred. She glanced at Mona and could see tears forming in her friend's eyes. "Don't pay any attention to her, Mona," Ashleigh said. "She's just trying to psych us out." She looked away quickly before Mona could guess that she didn't believe her own words.

Ashleigh gathered what was left of her lunch and tossed it in the trash. "My mom's picking me up from school so I can go to the feed store with her," she said. "Do you still want to ride together after school today?"

Mona nodded. "As long as we can work on show stuff."

Ashleigh knew the arena work would probably make Frisky worse, but what could she do? She had already tried to warn her friend. She agreed and left the cafeteria.

"How'd your day go, Ash?" Mrs. Griffen said when Ashleigh stepped into Edgardale's old feed truck later.

"Not so good, Mom," Ashleigh admitted.

Mrs. Griffen's eyes immediately filled with concern. "What's wrong?"

Ashleigh let out a deep sigh, then explained everything that was happening with Lisa, Mona, and the show.

"Hmmm," Mrs. Griffen said. "It always hurts when a friend doesn't believe that you want what's best for her." She paused for a moment. "I think you could be right about Frisky," she said. "Unfortunately, this is a lesson that Mona's going to have to learn for herself. So, to make things easier on the friendship, why don't you just go along with her for a while? There's no reason Misty has to go out on the trail. You could ride her in the front paddock with Mona." She smiled over at her younger daughter. "Besides, your father and I will feel a lot more comfortable watching you ride that big horse in the ring instead of out on the trail where we can't see you."

Ashleigh smiled gratefully. "Thanks for the advice, Mom. I hope Mona comes to her senses before Frisky is ruined."

They got to the feed store and spent their time looking at tack while the feed was being loaded. They drove back to Edgardale with the radio blaring.

Mrs. Griffen pulled into the stable yard and backed the truck up to the feed shed. "Go get Misty saddled, Ash," she suggested. "Mona will be here soon. Your father and Jonas and I will unload the grain and salt blocks."

Ashleigh ran to get Misty ready. This time she was

doing it all by herself. The kind mare stood still for her, but Ashleigh discovered that putting a saddle on a horse 16.2 hands tall was very different from saddling a mare that was only 14.3 hands. It took a lot of shoving to get her old saddle that far over her head. She had to stand on a bucket to put the bridle on the big gray's head.

At last Misty was ready. Ashleigh led her from the barn and out into the paddock. She pulled Misty up next to the fence and mounted from the top rail. Mona showed up a few minutes later.

"Come on in." Ashleigh waved to her friend. "My mom wants me to ride in the arena today."

Frisky and Misty sniffed noses, then fell into step beside each other as they walked around the paddock for a warm-up. On the second lap Ashleigh asked Misty for a trot. The mare's big, sweeping movements soon put her a half a paddock ahead of Frisky.

"Wow," Mona said. "Her trot looks just as good as Lisa's new gelding's. What's her canter look like?"

Ashleigh was a little bit afraid to canter the mare by herself, but they were in an enclosed area. Misty couldn't run off very far. She gathered her reins and smooched, giving Misty the leg cues for a canter on the left lead. Ashleigh was mildly surprised when Misty bowed her head and broke into a smooth canter. "She's doing it!" Ashleigh cried.

They spent several minutes practicing transitions

from walk to trot to canter and then back down again. After about twenty minutes Frisky began to act up. She purposely disobeyed orders and even kicked at Misty when she trotted by.

"Maybe we should stop for the day," Ashleigh suggested.

"No way," Mona said adamantly. "My trainer says if I quit on a bad note, Frisky will figure out she'll get to stop if she misbehaves. Let's do some small circles and work on bending."

Ashleigh asked Misty to turn in a small circle and tip her nose in toward the center. She used the reins and leg cues to keep the mare's body supple and moving in an arc. Ashleigh was thoroughly impressed with what Misty seemed to know.

Next the girls practiced side passes. Misty was a little rusty, but Ashleigh couldn't believe that the mare knew the move at all. "Wow," she said as she asked Misty to move on a diagonal, crossing her front legs over as she moved forward. "Maybe I should take her to the show this Saturday. Misty would give Lisa's new gelding a run for his money!"

Mona looked at her and frowned. "That'd be just great, Ash," she said sarcastically as she fought with Frisky. "You'd beat Lisa *and* me."

Ashleigh pulled Misty to a stop and took a deep breath. She was sick and tired of listening to these comments from her friend. Why was Mona being so rude lately? "With the way Frisky's been behaving lately, I probably *could* beat her with an untrained mare!" she blurted out in frustration.

The second the words were out, Ashleigh felt a flash of guilt. But it was too late to take them back—and maybe Mona would finally see how out of control things were getting.

"Well," Mona huffed as she made her way to the gate and let herself out, "you can find your own ride to the show on Saturday."

All Ashleigh could see was Mona's stiff back as she trotted Frisky down the driveway toward her own house.

Later that night the Millers called to see how their mare was doing. Ashleigh asked for a few moments to speak with Mrs. Miller about Misty. She told her about her experience with Misty in the paddock that morning.

"Yes, dear," Karen Miller said. "I probably should have mentioned that Misty's had a little dressage training, but I didn't think it would matter."

Ashleigh's eyebrows shot up. "Why would you give a racehorse dressage training?" she asked.

"Misty was a big two-year-old," Mrs. Miller explained. "We didn't want to send her to the track too early and risk hurting her, so we kept her home for another six months. She was always a kind horse, and since I was working on dressage with my show gelding, I decided that it wouldn't hurt Misty to try a little of it, too. She always seemed to enjoy it."

Ashleigh assured Mrs. Miller that Misty was once again enjoying the arena work and that the horse had settled in well at Edgardale.

"I just hope this takes her mind off racing for a while and that she can get excited about it again once she starts back on the track," Mrs. Miller said.

Ashleigh handed the phone back to her parents and went to finish her homework. But she couldn't get thoughts of the next show out of her mind. It was just a day and a half away—and it would be the deciding factor on whether she stayed in the running for the grand prize.

Mrs. Griffen drove Ashleigh to the show on Saturday morning, since Ashleigh and Mona still weren't talking. They arrived early and found a great parking place for the trailer.

"It's such a shame that you and Mona are fighting,"

Mrs. Griffen said as she backed Stardust from the trailer. "You two have been friends for so long."

Ashleigh frowned. "It's all her fault," she said. "Mona doesn't have to be so pigheaded!"

Mrs. Griffen raised an eyebrow. "It's *all* Mona's fault?" she said questioningly.

Ashleigh ducked her head and stared at the dirt beneath her black leather show boots. "Well, it's mostly her fault," she admitted. "I was only trying to help her with Frisky."

Mrs. Griffen handed Stardust to Ashleigh and pulled the tack from the trailer. "Sometimes these small problems blow themselves way out of proportion. It takes a big person to admit she was wrong and apologize," she said gently.

Ashleigh snorted. "Well, I don't think Mona will be big enough to say she's sorry." As she glanced up she caught the look on her mother's face, and her cheeks grew warm. Somehow she had a feeling her mom hadn't been talking just about Mona.

Stardust pricked her ears and nickered. Ashleigh looked up when she heard a return greeting. Mona was walking Frisky past with one of their friends from school. Ashleigh started to wave, but Mona turned her head and kept walking as if she hadn't seen her.

Ashleigh sucked in her breath. Even if she and Mona were having problems, how could her friend ignore her like that? She tightened her hands into fists. *Fine,* she thought. *If that's the way Mona wants things, then I'm happy to go along with it. I'm going to try my hardest today—and beat Mona as many times as I can!*

The ten-minute call came for the first class.

"I'll go register you while you get Stardust ready," Mrs. Griffen volunteered.

Ashleigh nodded and grabbed her saddle. She frowned when she saw that more of the stitching had come loose. She quickly tacked up Stardust and waited for her mother to return with her registration packet. As soon as her competitor's number was pinned to the middle of her back, she mounted up and headed for the arena. Lisa was just trotting up on her new gelding.

"Make room, girls, the winner is coming through," Lisa said mockingly.

Ashleigh worried that she and Stardust wouldn't be able to compete with the classy bay gelding, but after a few minutes in the ring with Lisa and her new mount, Ashleigh realized that the spoiled girl was having trouble controlling the big gelding. Lisa just couldn't keep Ranger collected, and she also couldn't seem to make him go into the correct lead.

To Ashleigh's relief, Lisa placed in only two classes the entire day. At the lunch break, Ashleigh counted her ribbons. She had one first place, a second, and a couple of thirds. Mona had won three of her classes and gotten a second place, but Frisky was once again starting to act up as the day wore on. Instead of scratching the mare, as she should have, Mona continued to fight with Frisky in every class, and the judges were noticing.

Mrs. Griffen handed Ashleigh a peanut butter sandwich and a soda. "You've done pretty well so far," she said as she eyed the brightly colored ribbons. "It's too bad Mona's having so much trouble with Frisky. She started out so well."

Ashleigh took a sip of her soda and stared toward Mona's trailer, which was just down the way. Mona sat laughing and talking with friends from her instructor's class. She acted as though not a single thing were wrong. "I'm worried about what Frisky's going to do in the jumping event," Ashleigh admitted. "I've never seen her behave this badly. Mona usually gives her a break, but she rode in all of her classes this time, and Frisky's getting worse with each passing class."

Mrs. Griffen pulled out a bag of chocolate chip cookies that Caroline had baked the night before. "Maybe you should say something to her," she suggested.

Ashleigh shook her head. "No way! Mona's already accused me of trying to trick her into pulling out of classes so that I could beat her," she said. "Maybe she'll do it on her own."

But when the call came an hour later for the green-hunter-over-fences class, Mona was lined up at the gate. Ashleigh could see that Frisky was upset. The bay mare rooted at the bit and pawed the ground.

The steward called them into the arena, and Ashleigh entered behind Frisky. The mare was acting up so badly that Ashleigh decided to ride past her. She was shocked when Frisky kicked at them as they passed, barely missing Ashleigh's knee.

"Be careful!" Mona yelled with an edge to her voice as Ashleigh rode past.

Lisa was the first to take the jumps. Ranger jumped the first hurdle almost perfectly, but his stride was wrong going into the second set of jumps, and he blundered through them. The next rider had to wait while the jumps were put back together.

When their number was called, Ashleigh steadied Stardust and circled the mare before heading for the first jump. "One, two, three, release, squeeze," she whispered to herself as she and Stardust flew over the low jumps. As she cleared the last hurdle, she knew that they had done well enough to place in the class. She circled Stardust back to where the other competitors waited.

It was Mona's turn next. Ashleigh watched as her friend circled her mare, trying to get Frisky's head down before heading into the first jump. The horse finally lined out and cantered toward the jump, but then faltered and dodged around the set of white rails. Mona righted herself in the saddle and pulled Frisky around in a wide turn, aiming for the jump again. This time the bay mare ran right up to the jump and bolted to the right at the last second, sending Mona headfirst into the rails.

Ashleigh gasped along with everyone else who'd seen the incident. She forgot all about the fight she was having with Mona as she slid off, tossed her reins to the girl on horseback next to her, and ran to her friend's side. Mona lay there, not moving. "Mona!" Ashleigh cried. "Are you all right?" She patted her friend's cheeks lightly. Mona's eyes fluttered open and she stared around as though she wasn't sure where she was. "Can you hear me?" Ashleigh said.

A second later the paramedics arrived and placed Mona on a stretcher. A large blond-haired man shone a light in Mona's eyes and checked several of her vital signs. "I think you may have to stay in the hospital overnight, young lady," he said. "You might have a serious concussion. The doctor will probably ask you to stay off your horse for a week." He looked at Mrs. Gardner, who had just run into the ring to be at her daughter's side, to make sure she understood the seriousness of the situation.

Mona shook her head and then winced in pain. "But

I can't take a week off," she protested. "I can't afford to lose any points!"

Ashleigh rocked back on her heels. Even after being in a serious accident, Mona was still worried about beating her and Lisa. What was the matter with her?

Mrs. Gardner flashed an apologetic glance at Ashleigh. "Mona doesn't understand what she's saying, Ashleigh. She'll be more clearheaded once she rests awhile."

Ashleigh glanced down at Mona's white face and felt a pang of fear. Mona could be really hurt this time. What if she had a major injury? Ashleigh's chest tightened. There was no saddle worth losing her friend or their friendship over.

She leaned toward Mona as the paramedics strapped her into the stretcher, preparing to move her. "If you have to take the week off, I won't enter the show next week," Ashleigh said. "You and I have the most points, Mona. If I don't show, you'll probably still be in the lead, even with a week off."

"You'd do that for me?" Mona said incredulously.

Ashleigh squeezed Mona's hand and nodded. "Our friendship and your being okay are more important to me than any stupid saddle," she assured her best friend. "You just get better, and when you're out of the hospital, we'll figure out a way for you to beat Lisa."

Mona grimaced as they lifted the stretcher, but she

managed a smile for Ashleigh. "I'll call you later if they let me."

Ashleigh watched as the paramedics loaded Mona into the ambulance. She realized that it didn't matter how badly she needed a new saddle. She needed her best friend even more.

11

Ashleigh visited the Gardners' house the following day when Mona came home from the hospital. She was relieved to find her friend sitting under a fuzzy blanket on the couch, watching TV. "Wow!" Ashleigh said in surprise. "I didn't think they'd let you out of the hospital this soon."

Mona shrugged. "I only had a mild concussion," she explained. "The doctor wanted me to stay overnight so she could keep an eye on me, but she said I was well enough to leave this morning."

"That's great," Ashleigh said, settling onto the other end of the couch. "Are you sore? You took a pretty bad fall."

Mona rolled her shoulders and moved her head slowly from side to side. "Just about every part of me hurts," she admitted. "Jamie invited me over to sit in her Jacuzzi later. My parents think that would be a good idea."

They sat in silence for a moment. Mona picked the fuzz off her blanket. Finally she looked up at Ashleigh. "I've been wondering . . . Why did you offer to pull out of the show next week?"

Ashleigh tilted her head to the side in confusion. "I'm pulling out so you don't have to worry about me getting ahead of you in points," she said.

Mona frowned. "When you said that yesterday I thought it was really nice. But do you really think that the only way I can win is if you disqualify yourself?"

Ashleigh didn't even know what to say. Where was Mona coming up with this? "N-no," she stammered. "Of course not."

Mona crossed her arms and looked out the window to where Frisky stood grazing in the front pasture. "Then what is it, Ash?"

Ashleigh shrugged, feeling very uncomfortable. "I was just trying to help," she said. "I know how much you want to beat Lisa, and you've been acting really weird whenever I do well in the show ring. What's the matter, Mona?"

Mona lowered her eyes to the blanket, refusing to meet Ashleigh's gaze. She was quiet for a moment. "I'm sorry, Ash," she finally said. "You *should* go to the show next weekend. I want you to keep showing Stardust," she said as she rubbed her temples. "Maybe I bumped my head harder than I thought, and that's why I'm feeling so strange."

Ashleigh sat in silence for several moments. Mona certainly was acting odd. This crazy competitiveness with Lisa was driving her to say and do such weird things. But she and Mona had been friends for a long time, and friends forgave each other. Mona was just going through a rough time. She'd get through it.

"Ash?" Mona said. "You have a strange look on your face."

Ashleigh smiled hesitantly. "It's nothing," she assured her friend. "I was just thinking about how we could fix Frisky so you can beat Lisa when you come back."

Mona picked up the television remote and lowered the volume on the TV. "I've been thinking about what you said last week, Ash, and you might be right."

Ashleigh waited for her to go on.

"You said that Frisky needed a vacation," Mona said. She drew her knees up and propped her chin on top of them. "Nothing my trainer has suggested seems to be working, and now the doctor's forbidden me to ride, so Frisky's going to get a vacation whether I like it or not. Maybe we'll try it your way. What do you think I should do?"

Ashleigh got ready to lay out her plan, relieved to be able to share her ideas without being yelled at for it. "Let's give Frisky the whole week off, with no riding," she began. "Next week we'll take the mares out and hand-walk them down the trail and let them crop the new grass for a couple of days. Then on Wednesday we'll do a nice trail ride back to the pond and let them eat grass again. We could do the same thing on Friday, the day before the show."

"But what about practice for the show?" Mona said in dismay. "If I'm going to compete, I need to practice."

Ashleigh sighed. "Come on, Mona. Have you really learned anything new lately?" She saw the confused look on her friend's face and continued, "It seems to me that all you and Frisky do is go over and over the same old things. That's why she's bored to death and acting up. I'm sure of it!"

Mona nodded slowly. "She does act totally different when we're out on the trail," she admitted. "And that's probably why she does really well in the first few classes at the show. Then she gets bored and misbehaves." Mona shrugged and gave Ashleigh a smile. "I've got nothing to lose. Let's do it your way."

The next week passed slowly for Ashleigh without having Mona to do horse activities with. But Ashleigh continued to work with Stardust and Misty.

Misty Flight was doing well with her arena work. Ashleigh was pleasantly surprised one day when Mrs. Miller stopped by to ride Misty herself. The owner was amazed that the big gray remembered so much of her earlier training. She even commented on the fact that Misty seemed to be developing a new attitude. Ashleigh invited the woman to come back and ride with her another day. At the end of the week she and Mrs. Miller took the mares out on the trail and had a great ride. It made Ashleigh miss Mona's company even more.

Ashleigh was glad when Saturday rolled around and she got to hang out with Mona again. She could tell that Mona was grinding her teeth at having to sit on the sidelines and watch, but she helped Ashleigh prepare for her classes and she kept a good attitude.

"I can't wait until next week, when I can start showing again," Mona said in exasperation. "I don't know how my mom can sit around all day and just *watch* me show. It's driving me crazy not to be able to be out there on Frisky!" She pointed to the arena, where Lisa was warming up on Ranger. The elegant gelding had his neck bowed and was moving nicely. "It's especially hard to sit here and watch Lisa show her new horse," Mona complained. "I can't believe she actually got a second-place ribbon in that last class!"

Ashleigh smiled as Mona helped her put shoe polish on the rough spots on her saddle. "I know it's hard, but just think—tomorrow you get to start walking Frisky, and in a couple of days we'll be out riding on the trails again! And next week you'll be back in competition."

Mona pursed her lips. "Lucky for me that Lisa is still having some problems with her new horse, and that nobody else but you seems to be winning more than one class." She sulked as she stared at Ashleigh's two blue ribbons.

"Don't worry," Ashleigh reassured her. "You're a great rider, Mona. You and Frisky will come back better than ever next week, and you'll do so well that your instructor will have to let you start showing dressage."

"Do you really think so?" Mona asked.

Ashleigh mounted up and prepared to enter her last class. "I *know* so," she said. "Even if I win this class, you'll still be one point ahead of me in the standings," she said. "Next week is the last show, and it looks like you, me, Jamie, and Lisa are all just a couple of points apart. It should be a good competition."

"Yeah, right," Mona scoffed. "It'll only be good if Frisky is fixed by then."

"She will be," Ashleigh said with confidence. "You just wait and see." She turned Stardust and headed for her last class.

On Sunday morning the girls took their mares out for a walk. Mrs. Miller had come earlier that morning to ride Misty in the front paddock, and Ashleigh invited her to go with them.

"It'll give Misty a chance to cool out and crop some grass," she said.

Mrs. Miller agreed, and the three horses had a nice leisurely walk in the fields with the whole countryside as their buffet table.

Later that week Mona saddled Frisky and met Ashleigh and Misty on the trail. Misty Flight was beginning to show some extra energy, and Mike thought it would be a good idea if she had a nice long trot on the trail. Frisky snorted and tossed her head, but Mona and Ashleigh could tell she was doing it out of sheer joy at being out on the trail again, not because she was acting up.

"This is great!" Mona cried. "Frisky feels like her old self again!"

Ashleigh smiled, glad to see Mona happy with her horse. She just hoped Frisky would hold her good attitude through the last show.

When they met again on Friday, Mona tried a couple of bending exercises and side passes as they roamed the big field.

"Don't do too much with her," Ashleigh cautioned. "You want her to feel like all of her show routines are interesting when she gets to the arena tomorrow."

Mona stopped her horse and dropped the reins low, allowing Frisky to lower her head to eat. She raised her face to the warm spring sunshine. "I forgot how much fun it was to just hit the trails and ride!"

Ashleigh leaned forward, wrapping her arms around Stardust's sun-warmed neck. She breathed in the heady smell of horse. "This is so great, I don't want this day to end," she said dreamily.

"But it has to," Mona said. "We've got to get to tomorrow so I can win enough points and finally beat Lisa at something."

Ashleigh felt a small flutter of concern, but she tried to stay calm. She'd told herself over a week earlier that this was the price she was willing to pay for her friendship with Mona. Mona would win the most points and get the fancy saddle. Ashleigh would just have to wait until the fall, when her parents could buy her a new saddle.

Mona glanced at her watch. "I've got to get back pretty soon. I have a ton of homework to get done tonight so that I don't have to worry about it this weekend."

Ashleigh sat up and pulled gently on the reins to lift Stardust's head. "Yeah, me too," she said. They reined the mares in the direction of Edgardale and started back at a leisurely pace. They rode in silence for several minutes. Then Ashleigh turned to her friend. "I've been thinking. Four of us are pretty close in points. I know you've got your heart set on beating Lisa, but I think I need to try to do my best in all my classes, too."

Mona looked at her with a bit of apprehension. "You're not going to bump me out of position at the last minute, are you, Ash?"

Ashleigh shook her head. "No, but if I'm wrong and Frisky does misbehave tomorrow, you won't get all the points you need. Wouldn't it be better if Jamie or I won instead of Lisa?"

Mona's lips fell into a deep frown. "I don't want Lisa to win," she said with determination. "And I really want to be the one who stops her, but I see what you mean. I guess it's better if we all try our best and the best horse wins."

Ashleigh felt her shoulders relax in relief.

"But," Mona added with a teasing laugh as she bumped Frisky into a canter, "I plan to be riding the best horse tomorrow!"

135

The girls laughed and settled down to race all the way back to Edgardale.

Ashleigh waved goodbye to Mona as she trotted into Edgardale's stable yard and dismounted. She took Stardust to the wash rack and hosed her off, then scraped off the excess water and walked her until she was cool. Moe was in the front pasture by himself and seemed to be upset about it, so Ashleigh turned Stardust loose with the little pony and went to do her chores.

"Are you ready for the big show tomorrow?" Jonas asked as he mixed the grain for the evening feed.

Ashleigh nodded. "Mrs. Miller will be coming by in the morning to ride Misty. I'll feed Misty her ration of grain early when I give Stardust hers, so she'll be ready to ride when Mrs. Miller gets here."

Jonas nodded. "I'll set up your morning feed tonight and leave it in the feed room next to the door." He pointed toward the front paddock with his mixing spoon. "Why don't you and Rory go bring your two horses in right now?" he suggested. "Your parents are going to leave the broodmares and babies out in the pasture, since the weather's supposed to be mild tonight."

Ashleigh called to Rory and handed him Moe's halter. The little pony was still kicking up a fuss when they went to halter the two. "I think you'd better start riding him more," Ashleigh warned. "He's way too hyper."

Rory fought with Moe to get the halter on his stout little head. Moe tossed his muzzle and stamped his little hooves, eager to be in his stall eating grain.

"Get him under control," Ashleigh said as she opened the gate to let Stardust through.

But Moe saw the open gate and made a lunge for it, dragging Rory off his feet. The little boy hit the ground with a thump and let go of the rope. Moe tore through the gate with a squeal and let his heels fly as he zoomed past Stardust.

Ashleigh heard the awful sound of hoof on bone as Moe connected with Stardust's shin. The mare tossed her head in the air and backed up rapidly, then stood with her leg lifted in the air as she angled her head down toward the injury.

Ashleigh felt as if Moe had kicked *her* right in the stomach. She dropped to her knees and inspected the injured leg, hoping that the pony had only grazed the shin, but Stardust refused to put weight on the leg, and Ashleigh knew they were in trouble.

12

"Ashleigh? Ash, are you okay?" Mrs. Griffen came running from the barn, yelling for her daughter. She scooped up Rory and directed Caroline to catch Moe.

"I'm sorry, Ashleigh," Rory sobbed as he stared at Stardust's swelling shin. "I didn't mean to let Moe go."

"I know you didn't," Ashleigh said as she continued to inspect Stardust's injury. The mare stamped her foot several times and then began to put weight on it. She took several hobbling steps, and Ashleigh let out a short breath. At least Stardust could stand on it, even if only briefly.

"I don't think anything's broken," Mrs. Griffen said as she ran her hand lightly over Stardust's leg. "But I bet it hurts like crazy right now." She brushed Rory off and kissed him on top of the head, then sent him to take care of Moe. "Give Stardust a few minutes, and then let's walk her into the barn and get some cooling liniment on it and wrap it for the night. She might be okay for the show tomorrow."

Ashleigh wasn't so sure about that, but she was willing to hope. She led Stardust slowly into the barn. By the time they reached the crossties, the mare was walking better, but the bump on her shin was getting bigger.

Mr. Griffen handed Ashleigh the liniment and a bandage. "Run a cold-water bandage on top of that so that it stays cool all night, Ash," he said.

Ashleigh nodded and began rubbing the menthol gel on her mare's leg. She soaked the outer bandage in cool water for several minutes before wrapping it around the leg. "That's it, girl." She patted Stardust and put her into her stall. "You've got to be better by morning. We've got to compete for that saddle!" She closed the door and went to the house to wash up for dinner. It was going to be a very long night.

Ashleigh was up early the next morning. She dressed quickly and ran to the barn to check Stardust. She pulled the mare from her stall and hooked her in the crossties, then carefully undid the leg wrap. The swelling had gone down, but there was still a slight bump on the shin. "Let's take you out and see how you travel," she said as she hooked the lead rope onto Stardust's halter and led her from the barn.

Ashleigh was encouraged that Stardust stepped out at a brisk walk. Maybe she wouldn't be lame and would be able to compete at the show that day.

"Good morning!" Mrs. Miller called when Ashleigh walked Stardust from the barn. She was just getting out of her car. "Are you ready for the show?"

Ashleigh shrugged. "Stardust got kicked last night, and I'm just bringing her out to see how she travels."

"Oh, no," Mrs. Miller said. "This is the last show— and the last chance you'll have to win that saddle!"

Ashleigh nodded, her heart sinking at the reminder. "Can you watch while I trot her and tell me if she's limping?"

"Of course."

But Ashleigh didn't even need to hear Mrs. Miller's report—she could tell from the second Stardust broke into a trot that the mare was faltering.

"Oh, dear," Mrs. Miller said. "There's no way you'll be able to ride that mare in the show today."

Ashleigh's shoulders sagged. So much depended on this last show. Even if she didn't win the saddle for herself, what if Lisa got it and made Mona's life miserable? She felt a tear slip down her cheek, and she reached to wipe it off.

"Wait a minute," Mrs. Miller said. "We've been

working with Misty, and she knows how to do most of the things they ask for in those classes. Why don't you take Misty to the show?"

Ashleigh looked up in surprise. "Misty? But she's a racehorse. Mike and Rhoda will be here tomorrow to gallop her on the track. Her big race is next week."

Mrs. Miller tipped her head and smiled. "Ashleigh, we won't be doing anything to hurt Misty. You'll be in a controlled environment with a fence around you, so she can't run away. And she's used to crowds. What's stopping us from doing it?"

Ashleigh frowned. "My parents."

Mrs. Miller smiled. "Let me worry about that. I'll go have a talk with them now. You just get your equipment ready to go."

Ashleigh looked at her watch. Mona would be there in another fifteen minutes. She quickly walked Stardust back to the barn and redid her bandage, then gave Misty her morning ration of grain and groomed the mare while she was eating.

Mrs. Miller showed up a few minutes later. "It's all taken care of, Ashleigh. Your mother and I will be going to the show with you. We'll follow the trailer in my car."

Ashleigh's face broke into a grin. "Oh, thank you so much," she said, beaming. Things were going to work out after all! She pulled the rub rag out of the grooming kit and polished Misty's coat until it shone. A few minutes later she heard the Gardners' truck pull into the driveway.

"What's this?" Mona said when Ashleigh led Misty from the barn.

"Stardust got hurt last night," Ashleigh explained as she loaded Misty into the trailer. "Mrs. Miller is letting me use Misty so I won't have to miss the show."

Mona crossed her arms in front of her chest. "But you'll probably win all the classes on that mare," she said.

Ashleigh stared at her friend, trying hard not to be angry. "I thought you agreed that if anything went wrong with Frisky, it would be better if me or Jamie won, rather than Lisa," she said. "What's going on with you?"

Mona glared at Ashleigh. "Oh, just forget it!" she said, and turned to get in the truck.

But Ashleigh could tell that Mona wasn't about to forget anything. "No, I'm not going to forget it," Ashleigh said. She grabbed Mona's arm, turning her back around. "What are you trying to say?"

Mona jerked her arm away. "You just want to be the best in everything, Ashleigh Griffen!" she blurted out. "Isn't it enough that you're going to be a great jockey someday? Why can't you let me be the best at what *I* like to do?"

Ashleigh sucked in her breath, stunned. "B-but it's not like that," she stammered.

"Isn't it?" Mona said as she turned on her heels and climbed into the pickup.

They rode in silence to the arena. Ashleigh noticed Mrs. Gardner shooting them worried looks, but Mona's mother didn't say anything. They pulled onto the show grounds and found a good spot, then unloaded the horses and prepared to tack up.

Ashleigh was hurt when Mona tied Frisky to the other side of the trailer instead of next to her horse the way she normally did. Ashleigh tried to ignore it and pulled her beat-up saddle from the trailer. She had to let the saddle's girth out several notches to accommodate Misty's bigger body.

The ten-minute call for the first class blared over the speaker system. Ashleigh finished tacking Misty and ran to the office to get her number. She couldn't resist running her hand over the beautiful saddle as it sat on its stand next to the registration table.

It would serve Mona right if I did beat her, Ashleigh thought as she remembered the rotten things Mona had said to her that morning. If Misty performed as well as she hoped, the saddle could be hers by the end of the day.

Mona walked into the show office to check in. Ashleigh turned and left before her friend could say anything. She needed to get Misty ready for the first class. She didn't have time to sit around and listen to Mona's hurtful accusations.

She reached the trailer and made the final preparations for her first class. When the five-minute warning came, she bridled the mare and mounted up, leaving ahead of Mona.

Misty pricked her ears and danced sideways as they cut across the show grounds toward the arena. Ashleigh hoped the mare would settle down by the time they reached the ring. The horses were just being let into the arena when she arrived at the gate. She gave her number to the steward and entered, feeling her hands shake as she looked at the big, empty arena ahead of her.

"Enter the arena on the rail at a trot," the steward called for the walk-trot class.

Ashleigh took a deep breath and asked Misty to trot. The big mare tossed her head and attempted to break into a canter, but Ashleigh quickly pulled her down to the slower gait. She could feel the power in Misty's stride as they passed several horses. She briefly wondered if the mare was beginning to get back her desire to compete on the racetrack. "Easy, Misty," Ashleigh crooned, but it wasn't until they had made several laps of the ring, passing several horses, that Misty began to slow her pace.

When the gray mare finally settled in, Ashleigh noticed that they were stuck behind Lisa and Ranger. Ashleigh grimaced as she watched the grand, sweeping strides of the classy bay. He bowed his neck and trotted around the arena with Lisa smiling her best as they passed the judge. Ashleigh felt helpless, knowing that she and Misty had already blown the class. Lisa was going to ribbon in this event, and Ashleigh would be left in the lineup along with the other disappointed competitors.

The judge asked for a reverse and a walk. Misty tossed her head in protest at having to slow down. When the call came to bring the horses in and line up, the mare was still fidgeting. Ashleigh knew there would be no ribbon in this class. Still, she gave the big mare a pat for her effort as they left the ring. She thought she saw a slight smirk on Mona's face when she trotted by on Frisky with a second-place ribbon in her hand.

Mrs. Griffen was waiting at the gate with Mrs. Miller when Ashleigh exited the arena. "Mrs. Miller thinks you should take Misty to the warm-up pen and work the excess energy out of her before your next class," she said. "I agree."

Ashleigh took the gray to the warm-up pen and put her into a canter, letting Misty determine when she'd had enough. The big mare cantered for five minutes before she offered to slow to a trot. Ashleigh walked her for several more laps, then went back to the arena to wait for her next class, which was only a few minutes away.

As they entered the arena for the English pleasure class, Ashleigh was amazed at the difference in Misty. She was also amazed that the judge's eye kept coming back to her. Ashleigh always had trouble in the pleasure classes with Stardust because the smaller mare's gaits weren't that smooth. But Misty looked like—and *was*—a pleasure to ride.

When the class was called in to line up, Ashleigh let out an excited squeal upon hearing her and Misty's names called for first place. Mona was right behind her with second place, and Lisa took third.

Ashleigh didn't enter the next class, and Mona and Frisky won first place. Lisa smiled haughtily as she gathered her second-place ribbon and Lynne took fourth place.

Ashleigh calculated the points in her head. They were all so close. If she won the English equitation class, as she normally did, she would be in the lead for the saddle. Mona would only be able to beat her if she won the jumping event and Ashleigh didn't even place. Because of an arrangement with another horse club over the loan of the jumps, the jumping events had been moved to just before lunch. The equitation class would be held after the noon break. By lunchtime Ashleigh would know if she had a chance of winning the saddle.

The stewards announced that there would be a fifteen-minute break in the schedule for the contestants to warm up over the jumps before the class began. Ashleigh buckled her helmet and entered the ring. They had set up makeshift jumps for Misty back at Edgardale, but the mare had never seen a real jump before.

Ashleigh took her time and let Misty sniff the new objects before she asked her to walk over them and then trot. By the end of the fifteen minutes, the mare was vaulting over them with only minor trepidation. But Ashleigh knew that her chance of placing in this class was slim.

The judges asked all contestants to enter the ring. They walked and trotted their horses, then waited at the side while the individual horses and riders made their runs.

Lisa and Mona both had almost perfect runs. Jamie and Lynne came close. There were several other riders who also did well in the class, and a couple who knocked down several rails. Ashleigh was the last to go. She gulped as her name was called, and she asked Misty to circle at a canter before heading into the line of jumps.

Ashleigh could feel the big mare hesitate as they came close to the first hurdle. She steadied her reins and put heavy leg pressure on the mare to keep her moving forward. Misty ran a little too close to the first jump before taking off, but she made a decent show of the next couple of jumps. Ashleigh smiled proudly and patted the mare when they trotted back to the lineup.

When the judge called out the winners, she wasn't at all disappointed with the fifth-place ribbon she received in the event. Lisa moved Ranger forward to accept the second-place ribbon. But she could tell by the look on Mona's face as she carried off her first-place prize that she was doing the math in her head—and that she knew Ashleigh and Lisa were the ones to beat for the grand prize. Mona would have to win the equitation class and Ashleigh would have to place fourth or worse in order for Mona to win. If Lisa won the equitation class, she would be the one to carry off the prize saddle.

Ashleigh took her time walking Misty back to the trailer. She wasn't looking forward to having to eat lunch with Mona and suffer the evil glares she expected from her friend. Ashleigh tied Misty to the trailer, preparing to do battle with Mona, but she was shocked to hear soft sobbing coming from the other side of the trailer.

"It's okay, dear," she heard Mrs. Gardner tell her

daughter. "I'm sure Lisa didn't mean to sound so harsh."

"But she did!" Mona insisted as she continued to cry softly. "We used to be friends, but now she lives just to make my life miserable. And Ashleigh's being horrible, too," she said. "She only brought Misty so she could beat me, and she *knows* how important it is that I win at this show. If Lisa or Ashleigh beats me, I'll never live it down. And worse, my riding instructor probably won't let me start competing in dressage. I'll never get to be a great dressage rider, and that's all that matters to me."

Ashleigh hesitated, wondering if she should let them know she was there. She knew she had a habit of eavesdropping—as Jonas loved to point out. But this time listening in just didn't feel right. She started to back away but stopped when she heard what Mrs. Gardner said next.

"I think this is all a big misunderstanding between you and Ashleigh," Mona's mother said. "I know you're upset, but Ashleigh's your friend."

Ashleigh held her breath, hoping the words would get through to Mona. It was so painful to hear her best friend say these things!

Mona sniffled. "Ashleigh almost always wins the equitation class." She blew her nose noisily. "I've worked so hard to be the best, but Ashleigh has as many points as I do, and she doesn't even care about being a dressage rider. It's not fair! And even if Ashleigh wins, Lisa will still tease me for not being the best. Ashleigh doesn't seem to care about that, either."

"Mona, are you sure this contest is worth losing your friendship with Ashleigh?" Mrs. Gardner questioned. "If you would just talk to her about why you're so upset, I'm sure you could clear this up."

Mona hiccuped. "It's too late now. Ashleigh's already mad at me. I can't take anything back."

Ashleigh grabbed Misty's reins and silently backed away. It broke her heart to hear Mona crying like that. But Mona was wrong. It wasn't too late to change things. She met her mother and Mrs. Miller at the show office and told them her plans.

Twenty minutes later, as she was watching the equitation class enter the ring, Jamie came up to her with a surprised look on her face.

"I thought you had to pull out of this class because Misty threw a shoe," Jamie said in confusion.

Ashleigh patted Misty as they stood by the fence peeking through the rails. "Right," she said.

Jamie studied the big gray's hooves. "But she's got all her shoes on, Ash. I *know* the farrier was busy with another horse. He couldn't possibly have put Misty's shoe back on by now."

Ashleigh shrugged, avoiding Jamie's gaze. But then

Jamie seemed to realize what Ashleigh was doing.

"You pulled out so Mona could win!" she blurted out. Then she frowned in confusion again. "But aren't you two fighting?"

Ashleigh pressed her lips together. "I heard your mom say you were leaving right after Lynne gets out of this class. Do you have enough room in that four-horse trailer to give me a ride?"

"Sure," Jamie said, obviously understanding that Ashleigh didn't want to talk about it any further.

The class lined up and waited for the results of the competition. Both Mona and Lisa did well in the class, but it was Mona's name that was called to accept the first-place ribbon. Everyone cheered, especially when the announcer said that Mona would be the recipient of the grand prize and that the Robbie Ward saddle would be awarded during an intermission after the next class.

"I'll meet you back at our trailer," Jamie said.

Ashleigh nodded and began to walk off. Suddenly she stopped and turned. "Jamie?"

Jamie gave her a questioning look.

Ashleigh removed her helmet and smoothed back her hair. "Don't tell Mona that I did this for her, okay?"

Jamie's brow furrowed. "Why not, Ash? You did a good thing."

Ashleigh kicked at the dirt beneath her boots. "Just don't, all right?"

"Sure," Jamie said. "But I don't understand you, Ash."

At the moment Ashleigh wasn't sure she understood herself, either.

13

Ashleigh stood on the rail at the Wortons' track as Misty trotted past. This was the mare's second gallop with another horse, and she was rooting at the bit, eager to run. Her race was in two days, and Rhoda was going to let Misty run during the last half mile to blow her out for the big race.

Mr. and Mrs. Miller stood on the rail, excited to see that their horse had returned to normal. Ashleigh tried to get in the spirit of things. Everything was going as planned. If Misty turned in a good work, she might be able to win the race. Then the Millers would have the fat purse, and Misty would come to Edgardale to live her life as a broodmare and raise great babies that would grow up to be just like her.

If everything was going so well, then why did Ashleigh feel so awful?

Because you miss Mona, a little voice inside her said.

Ashleigh knew it was true, but she couldn't bring herself to face her old friend after the way Mona had treated her. How could her friend not have trusted her? So she had hidden in her room when Mona had come to Edgardale, and she had refused Mona's phone calls despite worried looks from her mother. She wanted Mona to be happy, and that was why she'd stayed out of the equitation class at the competition. But at the same time, was she ready to forgive her friend for everything she'd said?

But you were *trying to beat Mona and win that saddle,* Ashleigh's conscience said.

Ashleigh had turned the problem over and over in her mind during the last several days. Her mother had insisted that the best thing to do would be to talk to Mona, but Ashleigh was still hurt and didn't feel like talking about it. The truth was, she was a little bit ashamed about her own part in all of this. She had been competitive in a field that had belonged to Mona.

Was she the one who had been a bad friend?

"Here they go," Mike said, bumping Ashleigh's elbow.

Ashleigh popped out of her reverie and focused on the two horses quickly approaching the half-mile pole. Three strides before the pole, Rhoda lowered herself over Misty's neck and asked the mare to run. Misty pinned her ears and dug in, challenging the other horse every step of the way. When they came down the homestretch, Misty began to pull away. She crossed the finish line a length ahead of the other horse.

Mike clicked the stopwatch and held it up for everyone to see. "It's not the fastest time I've ever clocked, but Misty was no slouch." He smiled broadly. "I'd say we're going to have us a real horse race come Saturday!"

Everyone applauded and congratulated one another. It seemed the vacation had done Misty good. There was just one hurdle left to clear now—the actual race itself.

Ashleigh cooled Misty out, talking softly to her and telling her how much she looked forward to being in the win photo for Saturday's race. It was only a couple of days away.

On Saturday Ashleigh was up early, feeding Misty her morning grain and making sure everything was ready to go. Misty would race at Churchill Downs in just a couple of hours.

The phone rang, and Mr. Griffen answered it. "It's for you, Ash. It's Mona."

He held the phone out to her, and Ashleigh felt her heart lurch. "Tell her I'll call her back after the race." She didn't want to add any extra stress to this day—she was already so nervous. A fight with Mona would just make things worse.

Mr. Griffen put his hand over the phone to muffle his words. "This has gone on long enough, Ash," he said sternly, and then held the phone out to her again. "You need to take this call."

Ashleigh picked up the phone, feeling her hands shaking.

"We'll load up in fifteen minutes, Ash," Mr. Griffen said as he picked up the hay net to take it to the trailer.

"H-hello," Ashleigh said softly, not sure of what she could say to make things feel less awkward.

"Ash, I'm so glad you finally answered." Mona's voice crackled over the phone line. "Listen, Jamie told me what you did."

Ashleigh couldn't tell if it was a statement or an accusation. Her heart squeezed. She didn't want to do this. Another fight with her best friend would be more than she could handle. She opened her mouth to tell Mona, but the words wouldn't move past the lump in her throat.

Mona spoke first. "I'm really sorry, Ash," she said, sounding as if she, too, was about to cry. "I put the competition before our friendship, and I shouldn't have done that. I've made a huge mess out of things just because I wasn't a big enough person to stand up to Lisa."

Ashleigh felt tears well up in her eyes. She still didn't feel strong enough to speak without it coming out in a sob. She held her breath, hoping the tears would go away.

"Ash?" Mona's voice was almost a whisper. "Are you there?"

"I . . . I'm here," Ashleigh managed to choke out.

"I want to make up," Mona said. "I don't like us not speaking to each other just because of a silly horse show!"

Ashleigh felt the tears slip down her cheeks. "Me neither," she squeaked.

Mrs. Griffen poked her head around the corner. "Ash, Mike's here. We've got to get going in a few minutes." She smiled apologetically. "Maybe you could invite Mona to go with us."

Ashleigh shifted the phone to her other ear. "Would you like to go to the races with us?" she asked. "We could talk at the racetrack while we're waiting for Misty to run."

"I'll have to ask my mom," Mona replied. "But I've got some chores left to finish. So if I go, I'd have to have my mother bring me later."

"Okay," Ashleigh said. "Maybe I'll see you there." She hung up the phone, still feeling funny inside. There were a lot of things they had to clear up, but at least they were making progress.

Mrs. Griffen came in to get Ashleigh, but she stopped when she saw the look on her daughter's face. "Are you okay, Ash?" she asked in concern.

Ashleigh nodded, and then she smiled. It looked as though things were actually going to be okay for her and Mona.

The trip to Churchill Downs was short. Ashleigh's breath caught in her throat when she saw the tall white spires of the grandstand come into view. Churchill Downs was home to the most famous horse race in the world—the Kentucky Derby. This year's Derby had been run the same day as the last horse show, but Ashleigh had been so depressed about Mona that she hadn't really enjoyed watching the tape of the race that Caroline had made for her. Maybe when she and Mona made up, she would pull it out and they could watch the Derby together.

Mike showed his ID to track security and pulled the horse trailer onto the backside of the racetrack, where all the Thoroughbreds were stabled.

Ashleigh never ceased to be amazed at all the activity and grandeur that went along with the backside of Churchill Downs. Everywhere she looked, grooms were busy in well-kept aisles lined with flowers and shrubbery, taking care of horses, hotwalking horses that had just come off the track, cleaning tack, or mucking out stalls. Many of the barns were decorated in stable colors, and expensive leather halters hung outside stall doors on brass pegs.

Ashleigh breathed it all in. Someday this was going to be her life, too.

"Let's get to work," Mike said as he pulled up to the barn. "I'll go check in at the track office while Ashleigh gets Misty ready. Remember," he cautioned, "no more food, and only a short drink or two of water before we run. We don't want Misty getting a belly cramp during the race."

Ashleigh hustled to get everything done and ready for the upcoming race. When the call came for Misty's race, her heart leaped into her throat. She had two more blue flowers to weave into the gray mare's mane before she was finished. "Hold still, silly," she said to Misty. Ashleigh was grateful when Mrs. Miller stepped into the stall to help.

Mike put the bridle on the mare a few minutes later, and Misty stood with her ears pricked, listening to the sounds of the horses being loaded into the gate for the next race. Ashleigh was glad she wasn't in the stall when the starting bell clanged because Misty snorted and rampaged around the stall, dragging the trainer with her.

"Whoa!" Mike said with a note of laughter in his voice. "I think this mare is ready to go!"

The horses were called to the back gate a few minutes later, and Ashleigh fell into step beside Mike. She knew she wasn't allowed into the saddling pen with him, so she slipped under the rail on the front side and went to stand where she had the best view of Misty. The mare looked great, and Ashleigh felt a twinge of pride in having helped get her to this race.

Misty tossed her head and pawed the ground as the saddle was placed on her back. Rhoda, wearing the blue-and-green silks of the Millers' stable, accepted a leg up from Mike, who gave her instructions for the race as he led Misty out to the track.

Ashleigh grinned at Rhoda's wink as the jockey passed, and then quickly ran to a spot on the rail by the finish line. The rest of her family and the Millers soon crowded in around her. She kept turning her head to look for Mona, but her friend wasn't in sight. Mona would probably miss the race.

"This is it," Mrs. Miller said as Misty trotted by, unaccompanied by a pony horse like the others in the field. The mare's muscles rippled, and the blue flowers stood out in contrast to her dark mane and tail.

"She looks great, Ashleigh," Mr. Miller said as he clapped a hand on Ashleigh's shoulder. "Thanks for all the hard work you've put into Misty. I know it's going to pay off today."

The horses finished the post parade and cantered off toward the starting gate. They were close enough for Ashleigh to hear the gatemen calling to one another as they loaded the nervous horses into the starting gate.

"Let's go!" the head gateman called. "Get that number two horse in there! Number three, you're next!"

Ashleigh held her breath as Misty was led into the gate. There were only two more horses to go behind her.

"They're all in," the announcer cried. "And they're off!"

The Griffens and the Millers screamed as Misty charged from the gate and vied for a place on the rail before they headed into the first turn.

"Arrow Star is in the lead, with Navigator running second, and Misty Flight is third as they head into the turn for this year's running of the Stanton Memorial," the announcer called.

The horses came out of the turn, and Misty began to move up the backside.

"Don't move her too soon," Mike said as he pulled his hat from his head and began twisting it. "You've got to save something for the homestretch."

But Misty continued to move up, taking over second place and challenging for the lead.

"Come on, Misty!" Ashleigh cheered.

The announcer's voice came over the PA system again. "As they move into the last turn, Misty Flight is now in command and running smoothly along the inside rail. Arrow Star drops out of contention, and Navigator moves up to challenge."

Ashleigh banged on the rail as the horses roared down the stretch toward the finish line. Navigator ran nose to nose with the big gray mare as they passed the sixteenth pole on their drive to the finish line.

Ashleigh thought she was going to pop from the excitement of the race. "Go, girl!" she hollered as she jumped up and down, screaming encouragement to the big mare.

Rhoda flagged her whip to get the gray's attention. That was all she needed to do—Misty's legs worked like pistons, and she began to ease away from the challenger.

"At the wire, it's Misty Flight by a length!" the announcer called over the roar of the crowd.

Ashleigh whooped and hugged Mrs. Miller and then her parents and Mike. Rory tugged on her leg, not wanting to be left out. Caroline lifted him so that he could hug Ashleigh around the neck.

"She did it!" Ashleigh cried.

Mike went out to collect Misty as she trotted back from the race, her sides heaving and her ears pricked toward the crowd. She seemed to know that all the cheering was for her. Mr. Miller herded everyone into the winner's circle for the photo.

Ashleigh watched as her parents shook hands with the Millers.

"It looks like you've got yourself a new broodmare," Mr. Miller said to the Griffens.

Ashleigh didn't think she'd ever seen her mother or father grin so widely.

Everyone made room for Misty as she stepped into the winner's circle with her nostrils flared wide. She stood with her head held high and proud. An official handed a beautiful engraved silver cup to the Millers and shook their hands as the speaker system announced them as that year's winner of the Stanton Memorial Cup.

Ashleigh smiled. Everything was perfect! *Well, almost perfect,* she reminded herself as a moment of sadness passed over her. Mona wasn't there to share in the fun of the winner's circle.

"Is everyone ready for the win photo?"

"Ashleigh!" a high voice called from the crowd.

Everyone's heads snapped around at the sound of the voice, scanning the crowd to see who was calling, but Ashleigh recognized the voice immediately. It was Mona. She'd made it!

The photographer called for everyone to look toward the camera.

"Wait!" Mrs. Miller cried when she saw Mona pushing through the crowd. She smiled knowingly when she saw the beautiful brown leather saddle that Mona carried.

Mona stepped into the ring and smiled broadly at Ashleigh, then handed her the prize saddle.

Ashleigh looked at her in shock. "What are you doing?" she gasped.

Mona shrugged. "Something I've been wanting to do all week, but you've been avoiding me. This prize belongs to you, Ash."

Ashleigh shifted the saddle in her arms, drawing in the wonderful scent of the expensive English leather. "But I don't understand."

Mona lowered her eyes and dug the toe of her shoe into the redwood bark of the winner's circle. "I had a lot of time to think this week," she started. "After the excitement of beating Lisa wore off, I decided that the victory didn't feel as good as I thought it would. Revenge isn't a good motive, Ash," she said, glancing up at her friend. "I was really a jerk to you these past few weeks, and I was only thinking of myself. But *you* put me first, even though we were fighting. You deserve this saddle. It's yours."

Ashleigh felt tears crowding her eyes. "But you can't just *give* me the saddle," she protested. "You won it fair and square."

Mona laughed. "I know what you did for me, Ash.

And maybe if Frisky hadn't been acting up, I *would* have won it fair and square. But you were the better rider. Take the saddle. It's yours, and I'm happy for you. Stardust will look great wearing it!"

Ashleigh hugged her friend as her family cheered.

"Everyone look this way for the win photo," the track photographer called.

Ashleigh looped her arm through Mona's and smiled at the camera. She knew that she and Mona still had some things to work out, but they'd get through it. That's what real friends did. She was happy to have the new saddle, but now she knew that the best prize was the friendship she shared with her all-time best friend in the world—Mona Gardner!

CHRIS PLATT rode her first pony when she was two years old and hasn't been without a horse since. Chris spent five years at racetracks throughout Oregon working as an exercise rider, jockey, and assistant trainer. She currently lives in Reno, Nevada, with her husband, Brad, five horses, three cats, a llama, a potbellied pig, and a parrot. Between writing books, Chris rides endurance horses for a living and drives draft horses for fun in her spare time.